THE

GILDED

CAGE

by

SORELE BROWNSTEIN

Dedicated to the loving memory of

Zeidy Yosef and (Super)Bubby Faiga Rodal, a"h

And Tova Gittel bas Esther a"h

ACKNOWLEDGEMENTS

It all started after watching a movie based on the Book of Esther. It was supposed to be a sweeping romantic love tale, but aside from the fact the characters were one-dimensional and unappealing, I was disturbed at how Esther was depicted: young, naive, and somewhat shallow. It occurred to me that, movie aside, it was fair to assume this was the picture most people have of Esther. Granted, she rose to the occasion by risking her life to plead for her people, but something gnawed at me. Is this the heroine we are meant to emulate? So she was a pretty face and charming... And therefore? I was raised to believe that our forefathers and fore-mothers, our biblical heroes, were spiritual giants whose lives were models to aspire to. If I found them to be lacking, the fault was not in them but in me. I needed to "wipe my windshield", so to speak, and discover for myself the truth our sages had transmitted.

When I first decided to shed light on who Esther really was and why she is deserving of our admiration, I thought I would tell the story from the viewpoint of a third person, perhaps a servant at the palace who could be "a fly on the wall" at all the crucial times. It was David Sutton (from the Blue Moon writers' group) who pressed me to write it from Esther's point of view. He felt, and rightly so, that it would be more compelling. I owe him a debt of gratitude. Initially, I was hesitant to do so, for how could I possibly speak for Esther? But as I strove to see things through Esther's eyes, basing her character on righteous, spiritual giants I have had the privilege to know, I came to appreciate and be inspired by her. I have learned from Esther simple but incredible tools for a freer, more integral life, to let go of control where you don't have it, and to trust that HaShem will take care of you. I finally understood ideas that I was raised with, to believe in Divine Providence, which I had only paid lip service to, but which Esther lived by.

I am grateful to Scott Evans and his Blue Moon Literary and Art group, for their encouraging support and helpful critique. Without it, this novel would read as I speak, like an immigrant fresh off the boat. Thank you, Howard Zochlinski, for introducing me to it. I am especially indebted to David Sutton, for patiently editing and re-editing my manuscript. I am blessed to be surrounded by friends and family who cheered me on, (Dini Polichenco, Devorah Leah Heidingsfeld, and Ari Kasowitz deserve a special mention) and most importantly, by a husband whose support is existential. Thank you to the Lubavitcher Rebbe and my parents for instilling in me the belief that our heroes were exemplary people worthy of our admiration, and therefore worthy of digging beneath the surface to find out why they deserve to be called heroes.

Blessed are You, HaShem, for granting me life and enabling me to reach this occasion!

TABLE OF CONTENTS

PREFACE

I was traveling on the train down the coast of Italy, admiring the green slopes, the worn stone houses, the white linens swaying in the wind. Wet laundry hung on strung lines out of small windows with crooked shutters. Inside my cabin, a well-dressed, middle-aged lady was sitting across from me. Hair gathered in a high bun, she wore a pinkish cream suit, with hands elegantly folded on her lap, legs crossed, and a somber expression on her face that gave little if any inspiration to start up a conversation. Also across from me, to my left, sat a haggard-looking man, prone to drinking, I assumed. Unshaven, sunken cheeks, mouth open, he snored, blissfully sprawled across two seats. As they were my only companions, and not being one to resign myself to just staring out the window for hours, I took out my Psalm book and started reciting the songs of King David, sottovoce.

"What's that you're reading? Is it Greek?" It was a thick, wine-coarsened, male voice.

The haggard fellow, now awake, was peering at me curiously.

"It's Hebrew."

His eyes lit up. "You're Jewish?" He looked like he had just encountered a rare mythical personality.

"Yes, I am," I answered, smiling, amused and, by now, used to this reaction by southern Italians.

His stunned excitement lasted a couple of seconds, after which he resolutely got up, sat next me, and with a conspiratorial air about him, began telling me how all the stories he grew up with about Christianity were not true and what he believed *really* happened. He grew more animated as he narrated Mary's indiscretions and her relatives' attempts to cover it up, oblivious to the murderous looks our traveling companion was firing at him.

He concluded his rant, and looked at me expectantly, waiting, I supposed, for confirmation, but I just shrugged my shoulder, at a loss as to how to respond.

The elegant woman across from me was wiggling in indignation, and could no longer contain herself. "How can you take a two thousand year old story, and... and *blaspheme* like that!" she spat, red in the face.

He turned to face her, eyes wide open, horrified that he was being unjustly accused. "But no, I *swear*!" he blurted out, right palm up, left hand on his heart. "I saw it with my *own eyes*! On *television*!"

It has been my experience that people will tend to read a novel or watch a movie, loosely inspired by a Biblical story, and assume that some of its details are factual. There have been countless movies and novels based on the Book of Esther, but none, I have felt, as an observant, deeply religious Jew, gave a proper voice to the Esther I have come to admire.

On the surface, the Book of Esther reads as a fable of sorts, filled with drama, suspense, and a happy ending. However, keeping in mind that it was written under the rulership and scrutiny of the king in

3

question, care had to be taken to tell the story without offending his sensibilities. The same methods by which the Jewish Sages have derived Torah laws from the text, a tradition passed down orally, have been implemented in the Book of Esther. Though I have taken creative license, I have drawn from our rich tradition: Talmud, Midrash, and commentaries by renowned Jewish scholars. I believe I have kept true to the values and character of Esther, but you don't have to take my word for it. I have included at the end the sources I have used, including what parts I have made up and what prompted me to those constructions. I invite readers to investigate and educate themselves about this fascinating story.

NOTE TO THE READER

Ever since the giving of the Ten Commandments, wherein it is stated, "Thou shall not take the name of – in vain", Jews have gone out of their way not to mention His name, if it could be helped. Hence, throughout the ages, He has been referred to as Master-of-the-World, The-Holy-One-Blessed-Be-He, Father-in-Heaven, etc... In the Book of Esther, His Name is not mentioned at all! In keeping true to the Book of Esther, I have endeavored to do likewise. I used the commonly used, in today's parlance, "HaShem", which literally means "The Name". When it could not be helped, I wrote it with a dash (G-d) in deference to the above mentioned custom.

FOREWORD:

A HISTORICAL BACKGROUND

The fourth century BCE was a dark time for the Jewish people. Gone were the glorious days of King Solomon, when all the nations had sought to ingratiate themselves with the G-d of Israel. Gone were the ten tribes of Israel, exiled and dispersed by Sennacherib, King of Assyria. The remaining Jews (because only the tribe of Judah was left, with minorities of other tribes, the children of Israel started to be identified as Jews) were dealt one blow after another. In 442 BCE, Nebuchadnezzar, King of Babylon, defeated the King of Judea, making the Jewish state a Babylonian vassal. At this time, he took along with him promising young scholars, such as Daniel, Mishael, Chananyah, and Azariah, to serve him. Only two years later, the prophet Jeremiah predicted the fall of the Temple, but the Jews refused to believe him. Six years after that, in 434 BCE, Nebuchadnezzar, in retaliation for the Jews' rebellion, plundered the Temple and exiled the king of Judea, together with the leaders of the Jewish people, among them, Mordechai.

In those years, Jeremiah and Ezekiel kept predicting the looming destruction of the Temple if the people refused to mend their ways, but they also promised that after seventy years, G-d would punish Babylon and rebuild the Temple. In 423 BCE, Jeremiah's prophecy came to pass; Nebuchadnezzar destroyed the Temple, and only a small number of Jews remained in Jerusalem. Now, all the Jews had left was the hope and promise that the second part of Jeremiah's prophecy would be fulfilled, that after seventy years, they'd return and rebuild (though many Jews started to assimilate to their life in exile.). There was uncertainty, however, as to the meaning of the seventy years. Was it to be counted from when Jeremiah first predicted the devastation? Or from when Nebuchadnezzar first exiled the King of Judea to Babylon? Or, perhaps, from the actual destruction of the Temple?

The Jews were not the only ones concerned. The kings of other nations still feared the G-d of the Jews, and made their own calculations to assuage their fear of reprisal from the Jewish G-d. Nebuchadnezzar reigned for another twenty-six years, during the last of which he suffered from extreme insanity, a reinforcement of the suspicion held by the gentile nations that there was no escaping retribution from the Hand of the G-d of Israel.

In the year 372 BCE, Belshazzar, a grandson of Nebuchadnezzar, calculated that seventy years had passed since his grandfather first conquered Judea in 442 BCE. Exhilarated that the G-d of the Jews had abandoned them, because there was no sign of their returning, he threw a banquet to celebrate, purposely using the Hebrew Temple's vessels as a sign of defiance. It was that same night that handwriting appeared on a wall, "*mene mene takeil upharsin*". Belshazzar was terrified and summoned Daniel to interpret the writing. It was Aramaic written in

Hebrew script, meaning "counted, weighed, and broken into pieces", which Daniel interpreted to mean that G-d had judged the King, found him wanting, and his kingdom was going to be broken and given away.

On that very night, Belshazzar was assassinated and Babylon conquered by Persia and Media.

Seventy years after Jeremiah first predicted the destruction of the Temple, King Cyrus, mindful of that prophecy, allowed the Jews to return to Jerusalem and rebuild the Temple. Unfortunately, because of libelous reports, and a setback in the economy, construction of the Temple was halted. Cyrus died soon after, and when Ahasuerus assumed the throne, he maintained the moratorium on building the Temple. In the third year of his reign, he calculated that seventy years had passed since Nebuchadnezzar exiled the King and leaders of Judea in 434 BCE, and like Belshazzar, he made a great feast to celebrate "victory" over the G-d of the Jews. It was at this party that G-d set in motion the events that would lead to the Jews' salvation. Vashti, the queen, was executed, allowing Esther to become queen in her stead. Five years later, she gave birth to Darius, who, in turn, at the age of eight, ordered the Temple to be rebuilt in the second year of his reign, seventy years after the fall of the Temple.

CHAPTER ONE

Now it came to pass...in Shushan the capital

(Esther 1:1,2)

"Ishtar! My beauty, how are you? What can I give you today?" Nashiram greets me with her usual exuberance, a plump middle-aged lady with deep dimples on her cheeks. She waves her ruddy arms around like a dance as she barks orders to her dependants; business has been busier than usual ever since the king threw a party for all the provinces in his kingdom. Shushan has been abuzz with so many different peoples and languages that I wonder if this is what it must have been like in the Tower of Babel.

"The freshest bream you have, please." I ask, trying to keep my voice from being drowned by the cacophony of the market. "Oh, and cinnamon."

"What do you need cinnamon for?" she objects, crinkling her sweaty face in reproach. She shifts her full weight onto the cart between us, sending a couple of wing-clipped doves on a protesting flight.

"I use it for the apricot *khoresht*," I venture timidly.

"Ah, no, Ishtar!" she thunders. "We Assyrian beauties need saffron; that is what we need!" she informs me resolutely. She wipes a dark curl sticking to her forehead with flair and, smiling magnanimously, as one would to a not-so-clever-child, she explains. "Cinnamon doesn't really agree with our digestion and it will make your complexion suffer. Trust me, you need saffron! Don't worry, I'll get you some," she reassures me with a friendly pat.

I smile patiently. There is no point in arguing with Nashiram; when she decides you are Assyrian, you *are*, despite what *you* may think. The certainty with which she passes down her declarations and recommendations is almost enviable.

"And the fish?" I inquire, hoping she'll agree that I need that.

"Yes, I'll have Rabona, my son, bring it to you later. The freshest!" she promises, bringing her fingertips to her lips and smacking them with a loud kiss. "Delicious!"

I thank Nashiram, turning to leave when someone catches my eye. Amid the hustle and chaos of the market place, she stands out because of her condition. Her lip is cut and swollen, dark bruises color half of her face and, my guess, most of her body, too, for she winces as she limps along her way. I wonder who could be so brazen and cruel as to strike such a sweet-looking girl so mercilessly and then shamelessly display his doing in public. She cannot be older than thirteen, small and frail, hobbling under the burden of her laden basket. Such a pitiful sight, yet no one seems to notice her.

I approach. "Can I help you? That basket looks very heavy!" I say, hoping she will realize that I mean her no harm and that my intentions are sincere.

Her dark eyes widen with fear. "No, No, it's all right," she says, shaking her head. "I can do it myself!" Her long, bony fingers tighten around the edges of her basket.

"I'm sure you can, yet I can't help thinking that some rest would do you good. Permit me to carry this for a little while?" Smiling, I lift the basket from under her arms. She reluctantly lets go, with a mix of fear and relief. All at once, I notice the royal emblem on her belt. I see now why she appeared to be invisible. I myself feel a little wary to interfere with the palace's affairs; nevertheless, she is a person, too, and deserving of compassion.

"What is your name?"

"Samanbar," she answers, her eyes downcast.

"Samanbar, can I ask you something?"

She looks at me questioningly.

"Oh, I was just thinking, I have this wonderful balm at home. It would do you some good. Would you stop by my house, so that I can give you some?"

She shifts uncomfortably and brings her hand over the bruised part of her face.

"It will only take a minute," I promise her.

She gives an almost imperceptible nod. We make our way through the dusty streets, leaving behind the dense smoke and pungent smells, breathing quiet air with relief. She keeps throwing furtive glances about her. I half expect her to run off, yet she clings to my side like a hungry puppy. We walk in silence until we reach my home, a modest little hut made of mud bricks. I invite her to come inside, but she declines. I insist until she finally enters, warily looking about.

I apply the mix of herbs as I have learned from Yasmine, the midwife. I always keep them handy, just in case there is a woman in need. I have been helping Yasmine for so many years now, bringing babies into the world, that I feel confident enough to do it alone.

I apply the balm gently on her bruises; she winces in silence.

"Why are you being so kind to me?"

I avoid her eyes and cautiously reply, "The question should be: who is being so cruel to you?"

She lowers her gaze and grimaces, trying painfully to avoid crying. I caress her raven hair. With the back of her hand, she wipes the tears that have made their way out despite her efforts, and sniffles. She couldn't have been in the palace too long: her pain is too fresh and she hasn't learned to quash her feelings and hide them in some deep recess of her soul. An experienced maidservant would have smiled and dryly informed me she was clumsy and prone to accidents.

"Who are you?" she asks in wonderment.

"My name is Hadassa."

Her eyes open wide. "You're Jewish?"

"Yes."

"Me, too!" she says excitedly. "My name really is Shulamit, but they call me Samanbar."

I squeeze her hand. Perhaps what attracted me to her in the first place was the familial connection.

"Shulamit," I say, looking her straight in the eyes. "Who did this to you?"

She darkens instantly.

"The queen," she whispers, cringing. Then, like a breaking dam, her tears start to pour.

"She…She. . ," Shulamit heaves. "She hates us Jewish girls…she makes us work. . Undressed…She humiliates us…'Where is your G-d now, why does He not come to rescue you?" She imitates a mocking tone, tears of anger now streaming down her face. "She laughs at us. 'Your G-d is gone,' she says. 'Defeated by my grandfather, the great Nebuchadnezzar!'"

"Do you believe her?"

"Shouldn't I?" she retorts defiantly.

"No, you should not," I answer simply.

"Why?"

"Because, although it is true that her grandfather destroyed the Beit-Hamikdash, our holy Temple, it is only because the Holy One, blessed be He, allowed it to happen, because of our many sins. But He promised us that after seventy years, He will bring us back and we will have the Beit-Hamikdash again."

"How do you know that?"

"Jeremiah, the prophet, said so."

"That may be so, but. . ," She hesitates. "Do you really believe that's going to happen? I mean, apparently seventy years have already passed..." She pauses, then drawing closer to me, she confides, "Some say that is one of the reasons King Khshayarsha is celebrating. What if they are right? What if G-d doesn't want us anymore?"

"No, even though a bad prophecy can be averted by repenting, a good one will always come true."

"How can you be so sure?"

"Do you believe in HaShem, the Creator of Heaven and Earth?"

"Yes."

"Then you can be sure, too."

She ponders my words.

"It's just that... Why is HaShem allowing this to happen? What have I done to deserve this?"

I embrace her. How does one answer such a question? I am no stranger to pain myself. My father died before I was born, my mother died in childbirth. No one wanted an extra burden, but Pethachia, my cousin, took me in. He was already an important leader, a member of the Sanhedrin, the Jewish court, as well as an officer in the Persian court, where he is known as Mordechai. He was not married but he raised me as best he could. Still, I missed the touch of a mother.

When Pethachia did marry, instead of seeing me as a little girl to adopt as a daughter, his wife, Deborah, saw me as a meddling sore, a rival, vying for Pethachia's affection and attention. She was jealous of my blossoming beauty, she resented the time Pethachia spent teaching me, and she made me pay for it. But I took it all in silence, for I did not want to cause Pethachia grief; he had done so much for me.

When she died about a decade later, Pethachia suggested I find a suitable match, for I had developed into a young woman, and he was old, and it would not be proper for us to live in the same household.

I smile when I think of his expression when I told him I had found a man that was G-d-fearing, humble, and virtuous, a great Torah scholar, kind, generous, uncompromising when it came to stand for Torah principles; would he agree to such a match? Of course, he had said. Then I told him it was he, Pethachia, I meant. Would he agree to marry me, for I could not see myself living with anyone else? He was taken aback at first, but by the grace of HaShem, he acceded at the end. Yet my happiness was marred by the fact that no child graced our home. For so many years, I prayed, I cried, and I still hope one day the Almighty will answer my prayer and bless me with a child.

I sigh as I collect my thoughts.

"I will tell you what my husband always tells me when I struggle with hardships."

She raises her soft brown eyes to me, thirsting for hope and comfort.

"Abraham, Isaac, Jacob, Rachel, Job, King David. They all had hard lives, HaShem tested them all the time, you know why? Because they were great, and HaShem knew they could pass their tests. Their challenges and suffering only made them greater, stronger." I take her hands into mine. "HaShem put you in the palace, in the hands of a wicked mistress. *You*, and not someone else. You can withstand this challenge, you can grow stronger from this. HaShem believes in you, He has great expectations of you."

We both fall silent for a while, contemplating the meaning of my words. Then Shulamit looks up at me and smiles timidly. "You know, it's odd that I'm talking to you about things I would never even dare say out loud to myself. How do you do that?"

"Do what?"

"Oh, I don't know, make me feel at ease, like you'll understand even if I say something sinful."

I kiss the top of her head. *Poor child, it must be terribly lonely in that idol-ridden place.*

Suddenly, Pethachia walks in, and at the sight of his stately bearing, Shulamit gets flustered.

"I didn't realize how late it was. I better go." She takes her basket and hurries for the door.

"I am sorry to have kept you so long," I say.

She takes my hand and kisses it with passion. "I will never forget you," she murmurs, and in a flash, she is gone.

"May HaShem guard you and protect you from all evil," I mutter to myself, staring out into the road that has swallowed her.

"A Jewish girl, maidservant to Vashti," I explain to Pethachia's questioning look.

He sighs and lets himself fall on the wooden stool. He looks fatigued, and *old*, as I have never seen him before.

"What is it?" I ask, pouring him some hot water in a clay cup.

He shakes his head sadly and sighs. I know the king's six-month-long celebration of his sovereignty has taken a toll on Pethachia, but this newly proclaimed week of festivity exclusively for Shushan's populace seems to be different. His pallor and the deep furrow that has formed on his forehead worry me. It is unlike Pethachia to be despondent, and if he is, it is reason to be concerned.

"ISHTAR!" A loud voice is calling from the outside. I remember Nashirams' promise to send me fish with her son. I step outside.

Rabona is brandishing a long silvery fish, smiling widely, revealing several missing teeth. "Mother says you are the only one who pays fairly without haggling on the price."

I pay the price he quotes and bring the fish inside the house.

"What are you going to do with such a big fish?" Pethachia asks, as he takes the fish from me and sets it on the table.

"Yom Kippur is coming and there are people who can use some food before the fast," I say as I ready myself to gut it. Fish can be quite slippery, so it takes all my concentration. I go about the messy task for a while, until I feel Pethachia's presence still hovering by my side. I look up to see him staring at me with a hint of a smile on his face.

"Ishtar?" he says with a twinkle in his eyes.

"It's what some people call me," I say, blushing.

"Like the goddess of beauty?"

My face and ears burn as I blush furiously.

"I suppose I can see why they would deem that name appropriate for you."

"Hadassa is fine by me," I reply quietly.

"Indeed. Hadassa does suit you, for your deeds are pleasant as the scent of the *Hadas*, the fragrant myrtle."

"So how was it, at the palace?" I ask, embarrassed, eager to change the topic.

Pethachia sobers, and lets out a deep sigh. "Regrettably, what I had feared is happening. Though the Jews' motive in attending the party was only out of fear of King Achashverosh, once they were there, they fell prey to the temptations of the occasion and are now actually partaking of, and enjoying it." Two lone tears slip silently down Pethachia's cheeks as he continues, his voice hoarse. "They are desecrating the holy vessels of the Temple and that wicked Achashverosh is wearing the priestly garments..." He clutches his head with his hands and starts weeping. "Woe to us, for we have sinned!"

His burst of anguish tugs at my heart. I know he must be reliving the traumatic destruction of the Temple and the exile. I watch him helplessly, wishing his pain away. And to think we had come so close to rebuilding the Temple! King Cyrus allowed us to return to Jerusalem and rebuild, only to rescind his decision because of the malicious libels of Jew-haters. I suspect that conniving minister, Haman, had a hand in it. King Cyrus died soon after that, and when, later, Achashverosh, through sheer ambition, wealth, and intrigue, acquired the throne, he prohibited any further construction. He is an arrogant man who desires supreme control and fears the G-d of Israel will prevent that. Come to think of it, he and Vashti suit each other well, both being physically and ideologically descendants of the wicked Nebuchadnezzar.

"Restore us to You, oh, HaShem," Pethachia cries, his hands raised heavenward. "That we may be restored! Renew our days as of old."

"Amen," I reply fervently. "May it be His will."

CHAPTER TWO

I will surely hide my face

(Deuteronomy 31:18; Chullin 139b)

I take a deep breath and let the crisp air of dawn caress my face. I love this time of day, when the city is mostly still, and the birds' songs are unmolested by vulgar human clatter. It holds promise and it is vibrant, like the spirit of youth.

The Holy Days are past us, the winter months are rolling by, and yet, Achashverosh's party and its bloody aftermath are the only topics on everyone's lips.

Rumors abound, though it is impossible to discern the true from the embellished, from the outright fabricated. What remains certain is that the queen is no more. How, and why? I cannot say it concerns me very much. That Achashverosh may be fickle surprises no one; what has the whole Empire befuddled is how trivially the king had his queen, a woman of powerful noble descent, summarily executed. It doesn't bode well for her successor.

Tamar and I are drawing water at the Ulai river, placing the casks on Tamar's mule.

Our hands are purple, numbed by the frigid waters, but we are too engrossed in our conversation to care.

"I mean no disrespect to Mordechai, but we were right to go!" asserts Tamar, who has been trying to win me over to her side. "See what happened to Vashti when she displeased the king? It did not help her to be queen and a daughter of royalty. Can you imagine the consequences, had we not attended?"

"I am not one to engage in arguments, but it seems to me that Vashti was punished not so much because she disobeyed the king, but because HaShem saw fit to punish her for her wicked deeds." I have not forgotten Shulamit's bruised face. "And what Petha... I mean, Mordechai said still holds true, we should not have gone. They dishonored the Temple and HaShem, and for us to just stand by or dismiss it is wrong!" Blood rushes to my face. It is a topic I feel strongly about, one that keeps coming up in the wake of this great insult to our heritage. And it feels particularly close to home, when I see it personified by my own close friend and neighbor, typifying an alarming growing apathy to our roots as a people.

"Why must you and Mordechai persist in your obstinate ways? You have to come to the realization that HaShem exiled us. We are not in our holy land anymore, therefore, we need to conform."

"HaShem may have exiled our bodies, but not our souls! We cannot lose sight of who we are as a people. We are different."

Tamar shrugs. "I don't see it that way. Hadassa, you're beautiful, you're married to one of the leaders of the Jewish people. To you, everything is simple, black and white, but life is more complicated than that."

"We have the Torah that helps us navigate life's complications." I pause to allow my words to sink in. "I believe all the sages were in agreement regarding Achashverosh's party."

Tamar snickers. "Ha! Tell that to all the ministers who were hanged because they had advised the king to kill Vashti after she had slighted his honor." She shakes her head. "Achashverosh is a lunatic! Had we not gone, he would have taken offense, and who knows what he would have done? One should not rely on miracles, is that not true?"

"One should follow the Torah. And the Torah tells us to follow our sages' advice."

"You make it sound so simple: follow the Torah, good life; be wicked, bad life. But it's not like that. That hateful Haman miraculously escaped death and still holds his position of advisor to the king."

"Certainly there is a reason the Almighty saw fit to spare Haman."

"Certainly! If only I could fathom His reasoning…"

I ignore her sarcasm as my mind is otherwise preoccupied. Haman is not an opponent to dismiss lightly; undoubtedly, having so many sons holding royal positions, he must have arranged for his noose to be tampered with so that when his execution came, he fell from it, thereby saving his life. Not only does the law grant life if one "survives" execution, but now rumors are going around (no doubt started by Haman himself) that the gods find favor with him, for he truly had the king's honor at heart. I wonder what he is scheming next.

"Certainly, he's keeping his distance right now…" Tamar, unaware that my mind has been wandering, is still pontificating on the unfairness of life. "But I'm sure sooner or later, he'll find a way to either ingratiate himself completely with the king or, perhaps, even do away with him."

Tamar lifts her double chin defiantly, daring me to counter her logical conjectures. I smile inwardly. One of the things I appreciate about her most is her openness and unabashed habit of letting you know what is on her mind. It is a challenge I welcome.

I still stand by my conviction. It *is* simple. Jews without Torah cannot survive as a people. We would blend and assimilate to become completely forgotten. But simple and easy are not synonymous. Of course there are evil people who have good living. Moses himself questioned HaShem, "Why have You done bad to this people whom you profess to love?" Yet there was no response. HaShem is Unknowable. That does not mean that He does not care for us or does not wish our well-being. We are not always privy to the answer of all our questions; that is the beauty of faith.

Tamar takes my silence as a sign she has won the argument. A smug smile spreads across her face. To her, having the last word is of paramount importance. I can only hope that one day, she will accept the truth of my words.

We near our humble mud-brick homes.

"You know, Leah is due to have a baby at any moment. She's been complaining of pains in her legs.

Do you have something for that? She prefers you be there when it's time, you know."

"I'll go see her as soon as I have a chance."

I set down the casks to kiss the *mezuzah*, the rolled up scroll laid in a hole on the doorpost of my home. "I may have to go to the market. I am missing some cumin and other herbs; Nashiram will be able to procure them for me."

Rough fabric is hoisted on wooden beams in an attempt to provide some respite from the glaring sun. People's wares are displayed in their carts or on the ground. There are those who shout to catch the attention of the passersby, and those who sit sprawled next to their wares, distracted by the commotion around them.

I make my way to the familiar spot where I am sure to find Nashiram. She is still harping on the law that was passed recently by King Khshayarsha, the one that decreed every woman is to submit to her husband. It is not as if it was different before, so why the law?

"I should stop speaking Chaldean to my children, or my husband is obligated to report me and I would face death? Have you heard anything so insane? I told my husband no such thing shall ever happen, he adores me too much, and I certainly shall not stop speaking Chaldean! Why, that was my parents' tongue and my children should know where they come from. Besides, knowing more than one language can only be beneficial! It's the most ridiculous law I have ever heard of!" Nashiram's passionate rant is directed to no one in particular, but she is confident everyone must be captivated. Indeed, she is masterful in the art of drama.

She lowers her voice with an air of importance. "Now, I have ties to the palace; my cousins have been working in the king's kitchens for generations, and they tell me," She raises her brow for effect, her eyes brimming with meaning. "Vashti may have been beautiful and from royal blood, but she was poisonous as a snake. She received what she deserved, why should *we* have to suffer?"

I half-nod my "agreement" while I select the herbs I need.

"I can only hope the king will have better sense with a new and better queen." Nashiram winks, but whatever she might be implying is lost on me. Nashiram is disappointed by my reaction, or lack thereof, but only for a minute. Undaunted, she persists. "You know, Ishtar, one may never know who the next queen might be."

I stare at her stupidly.

She beckons me to come closer. "I hear rumors… they are searching for beautiful girls," she whispers. "The other day, someone asked me who I thought was the most beautiful maiden in Shushan, and I, of course, said you, my Ishtar!" she exclaims gleefully.

I am dumbfounded. Nashiram pats me on the back as I stammer some incoherent goodbye.

I make my way home, my heart in a vice, with a sense of foreboding I cannot shake off.

I have decided to heed my gut feeling and keep inconspicuous, not leaving the house for any reason. It is a decision Tamar has yet to accept. She stands at the doorway, holding the herbs I just gave her, scowling at me.

"I just can't understand why you wouldn't come. You know Leah would rather have you!"

"I'm sorry, I really am, I just—" I let out a deep sigh. "I think I should stay home for a while."

"And what? Hide like a thief? Until the king finds himself a new queen? You can't be serious, Hadassa!"

I shrug. I do not know what to say. I *am* serious.

"Don't you think you are being a little presumptuous? Don't get me wrong, you are beautiful, and you may look young, but you can't compare yourself to a truly young girl! Besides, you're married, and they are probably looking for maidens, you know."

I want very much to believe her. I have repeated the same arguments to myself countless times, yet the uneasy feeling persists.

Tamar shakes her head, disappointed in my decision to stay inconspicuous. She shrugs and turns to leave.

"Will you help me, Tamar, please?"

She gives a slight nod. "I'll pick up what you need," she mutters.

*   *   *

The rolling hills surrounding me are dry. Shades of yellow dotted sporadically by streaks of green. I am not in Shushan. Still, it all looks vaguely familiar. The sun, perched high in the sky, is beating down mercilessly. The stench of sweat mixed with dirt and blood is all the more intense because of the heat. There are people around me, yet they do not seem aware of my presence, as though I am there and not there at the same time. It is all very vivid, but I know I am dreaming.

A tall, handsome man approaches, gripping a sword. His robes suggest that he is a Jew of royalty. He raises his sword, poised to strike. Facing him, huddled on the ground, bruised and bleeding, is a man in tattered crimson robes. He spits black phlegm on the ground, and pleads for his life. The tall man wavers, lowering his sword. No sooner does he set the sword at his side than the huddled supplicant turns into a horrid snake and strikes at him with a vengeance.

"AAAHH!" I wake up with a start, my voice still reverberating in my throat, pearls of cold sweat trickling down my forehead.

"Hadassa, are you alright?" Pethachia is hovering over me, a tremulous candle in his hand, staring at me with a concerned look on his face.

I nod, still trembling.

He places the candle back on the table, unrolled scrolls lying across it, and he brings me a basin and a pitcher of water. I wash my hands to remove the impurities that sleep brings.

"Just a bad dream," I say, trying to reassure him, but failing miserably. "I am sorry for having disturbed your learning."

He waves his hand to dismiss my concern. "You have been sleeping restlessly these past few months. You do not go out anymore, even to help women the way you used to." He lets out a deep sigh. "Tell me about the dream," he asks, his voice gentle but firm.

"I am watching a Jew, perhaps a king, about to execute a heathen. He hesitates because he feels pity, and the heathen turns into a beastly snake and strikes at him. And strikes, and strikes, and the king is lying on the ground...and he is looking at me and pleading for me to help him—" I relive the impact of that gaze for a moment and shudder. "Then I wake up."

I look up to Pethachia, hoping he will laugh it off as nonsense, but his brow is furrowed and he looks troubled.

"What do you think it means?" I breathe.

He strokes his long white beard. "I am not sure. What do you think it means?"

"Perhaps it is just meaningless," I venture. "I became overly apprehensive when Nashiram told me about the king's agents searching for pretty maidens…" My voice trails off, I want so badly for Pethachia to tell me that I am overreacting. Instead, he nods gravely.

"Perhaps," he says, unconvinced.

Now I am truly alarmed. He must know something he is not telling me. And I haven't even told him that the eyes I stared into, the ones that implored me to help, they were my own.

I splash some water on my face and wipe the copper mirror. My eyes stare back at me. I could never quite define what color they are, green or gray, with specks of yellow and orange, framed by a thick, black outline. They are quite uncommon eyes, so it presses me even more to know: who is that man in my dream, why does he have my eyes, and what is the meaning of it all?

*   *   *

Tamar bursts into my home, exasperated.

For the past three years, she has begrudgingly resigned herself to my stance, though she never missed a chance to remind me of her contention with me. This time, her mood is different, she is agitated and her words are tumbling out incoherently.

"This is unsustainable, it is incomprehensible!" She looks at me and shows me the palms of her hands. "I know, I know, you were right! It pains me to admit it, but the situation cannot go on like this, unbelievable!" She plops down on a wooden stool, which creaks under the force of her angst.

"What is the matter? What are you talking about?"

"What's the matter?! Have you not heard the new law? Has Mordechai not told you?" she retorts incredulously, her face turning dark hues of red.

I shake my head confused.

"You know how I thought you were being ridiculous for thinking they would take you as a contender for the king?"

Yes, I know.

"But you were right. Rumors are running wildly that it's precisely you they are looking for, and they won't stop until they find you!"

"What do you mean?" I stammer, my gut clenching.

Pethachia's deep voice catches us both by surprise.

"It means that what I was afraid of is true. You cannot escape your destiny."

Tamar almost falls off her stool. She bows several times with reverence. "Peace unto you, our master, our teacher, may you live long," she whispers with awe.

I forget myself for a second and suppress a smile. Tamar has never had any qualms about criticizing my husband, how he ought to quit parading his Jewishness, our differences, for it makes the Persian people uncomfortable and irritated. Though I suspect she means herself more than the Persians. "It's causing people to hate us," she claims, but I cannot disagree with her more. Whatever her harsh position on Pethachia's attitude, whenever she is in his presence, her demeanor transforms completely. Gone is her arrogance and a timid Tamar looks on with admiration.

Pethachia acknowledges Tamar with a slight nod, and then turns to me.

"Hadassa, I always knew you were destined for greatness." he says softly, his eyes moist. "Now I do not know exactly why it is, but I believe it is HaShem's plan for you to become queen."

"What could I possibly accomplish in that idol-cove that I cannot accomplish here with you?"

Pethachia hangs his head. "I do not know," he whispers.

"I do not want to go."

"I know."

"Forgive me for interrupting," Tamar ventures. "But I must say this."

She approaches me, and takes my hands into hers. "Hadassa, the king has passed a new law that any man found harboring a beautiful maiden shall be hanged at the door of his own home. Our revered sage, Mordechai, is putting his life in danger every day that he keeps you here. Can you live with that?" she asks softly with a sweetness I never heard from her before, her eyes brimming with tears.

"No."

"Then go out into the street, and start walking. If you are taken… then, well, aren't you the one who always says everything is from HaShem?"

I stare at the floor in silence.

"And aren't you the one who says that HaShem only wants what's best for us?"

It is hard to believe I am hearing this from Tamar's lips.

"You are right," I say, fighting away my tears. "I have been lacking in my trust in HaShem. Perhaps the sooner I overcome whatever challenge awaits me, the sooner I will be set free. " I look Tamar in the eyes. "Thank you."

She nods. "My mother, may her memory be a blessing, used to say, when telling us the story of

Moses, that you don't ask for greatness, greatness is cast upon you. And I cannot think of a better-suited person for whatever HaShem has in mind than you."

I give her hand a tender squeeze.

"Will you please give us a moment?"

She bows and scurries away, while sniffling and wiping her face with her arms.

I turn to Pethachia. His face is ashen. "Pethachia…" I choke.

"Shhh, Hadassa, do not cry," he says, his voice heavy with pain. "HaShem's reasons are hidden from me right now, but I know greatness awaits you."

I nod imperceptibly.

"Hadassa," Pethachia draws near me. "I need you to promise me that you will not tell a soul who you are or where you come from."

I search his eyes, kind eyes that seem to disappear within the crinkles of his dear face.

"I believe it is important to keep it a secret. Achashverosh is no lover of Jews…" His voice trails off.

"I promise you, Pethachia, on everything I hold dear and sacred."

"And when people ask you what your name is, tell them it is Esther, for though it is a Persian name, it is appropriate for you because in Hebrew, *seter* means hidden, HaShem has concealed Himself from us, and we stumble in darkness."

"And I will be concealing who I am."

"May HaShem protect you and guard you."

"And may I be reunited with you soon."

"Amen, may it be His will."

With a heavy heart, I turn to leave.

"Hadassa!"

I turn around. Pethachia's face is flushed. He does not say anything but he gazes at me intensely, teary-eyed. He does not need to say anything, I understand. I return his gaze and, silently, I tell him all the things words cannot express.

"Esther." I reply, a bittersweet smile on my lips.

I hold his gaze and search his face, thirstily drinking in every detail, wishing to impress on my memory every groove and every wrinkle.

I tear myself away and turn to go.

Outside, the sky is clear, but inside, my heart is storming. My mind is numb, yet my feet carry me with resolute steps, with a will of their own.

I dare not turn around, but I can feel Pethachia's gaze following me.

CHAPTER THREE

And Esther obtained grace in the eyes of all who beheld her

(Esther 2:15)

"You, woman!" A gruff voice jolts me out of my trance. "Where do you think you are going?"

My legs have suddenly turned to stone. I keep my eyes glued to the ground. The sound of approaching steps sends my heart on a galloping frenzy. The shadow of a guard, with its unmistakable fluted hat, looms ominously.

"Where are you going?" he demands.

"I…I am going to the market," I say when I finally find my voice, keeping my face down, staring at the ground.

"The market?" the guard asks, perplexed. "Have you not heard of the king's proclamation? Who is your guardian? Why are you not at the king's palace?"

"I assume the law does not apply to me, being that the king is looking for young maidens."

My reply is met by a roaring guffaw. Before I have a chance to anticipate his next move, he grabs my arm in a firm grip and pushes me unceremoniously into a stumbling walk.

Terrified and dizzy, my limbs are limp and so is my mind. Hard as I try, I cannot form a single rational thought.

At the palace's gates, my kidnapper's grip remains unrelenting. I see many women walking, some eagerly, some less so, as they are directed to the right of the palace's western entrance, where two enormous, stone, man-headed bulls preside.

I assume I will be brought together with the other women, but the guard brings me to another section of the palace.

"Call the king's eunuch, Hegai," he announces to the servant at the door. "We found her."

Found her?

A short, round man comes puffing through the chamber. His head is shaven and his skin is smooth as a baby's.

"Why have you not brought her together with the rest of the girls, in the Harem, for quarantine?" he demands with a high-pitched voice, pulling himself to his full four feet.

"She's the one of whom the rumors abound. You only need to look at her to realize that she is worthy to be queen."

I am surprised that, notwithstanding his conviction that I am suitable to be queen, it did not deter him from fetching me in a not-so-royal fashion.

Hegai surveys me. "Indeed," he muses. "I can see what you're saying."

"It was I who brought her to the palace!" the guard insists, like a hunter demanding his reward for bringing in the finest catch.

Hegai eyes him knowingly. "Very well, I shall remember that."

"And what might your name be?" he asks amiably, turning to me.

"Esther."

"Esther…from?" he prompts.

"Esther from Shushan," I answer.

"Yes?"

He is expecting more details, I know, but I cannot give him that.

I remain silent.

Hegai clears his throat. "Well, let's proceed then, shall we? Welcome to His Majesty, King Khshayarsha's, magnificent abode!" he declares with a wide, sweeping motion of his arm.

He may be King Khshayarsha to you, but I cannot think of a more apt name than what we Jews have come to call him.

Achashverosh has been nothing but an ache, pain, in the rosh, head, for us.

"…You will be made to feel as a queen as long as you will be in my care and under my tutelage, you'll be missing nothing. The king has ordered for your every wish to be…"

Hegai's shrill voice weaves in and out of my attention as we make our way through courtyards and chambers. Luscious gardens, imposing marble pillars adorned with ivory bulls, elaborate, colorful reliefs, alabaster pavements covered by gold-woven carpets. The opulence is overwhelming, and the presence of idols everywhere unnerving, suffocating. It is a veritable prison. I wonder how long I will have to endure it to fulfill whatever mission HaShem has in store for me.

"Is there anything in particular you wish for?" Hegai's question hangs in the air as he awaits my reaction. Three servants are by his side, holding platters of jewels, and colorful, shiny dresses.

"You're very kind, but no, thank you, I wish for nothing."

Nothing this palace has to offer.

Hegai is stunned and apparently moved by my response.

"But, my dear, you need not be shy. The king has ordered every maiden's whim to be accommodated."

"Then I have no whim."

My reply is met by a stunned silence.

"Follow me," he finally says, shaking his head in disbelief.

We come to a vast and ornate chamber. Drapes of green and blue hang above us, held fast by silver rings and purple ropes that coil sinuously down the marble columns.

"Here is where you'll stay until your turn to meet the king comes," Hegai announces, spreading his arms as if in invitation.

May my turn never come.

He claps his hand and barks a few orders to the servants in his soprano voice.

"You will want for nothing, milady. I have called for Vashti's former personal attendants to be summoned so that they may serve you. In the meantime, you must be hungry, so please help yourself to the finest foods the palace has to offer."

Servants appear, carrying golden platters filled with all sorts of delicacies. Soon, the chamber is filled with the sickeningly sweet smell of roasted meats and aromas of delicacies forbidden by our holy Torah.

I feel the blood drain from my face, but I maintain my composure.

"If I may…"

Hegai turns to me.

"You have been very kind to me, and the food does look enticing…but I am afraid I am not accustomed to eating such delicacies, and it might upset my stomach. I would be eternally grateful to you if you would indulge me and allow me to keep to a diet based on raw fruits and vegetables."

Hegai eyes me hesitantly. "I suppose it can be done…" he says, scratching his shiny head. "Seeing that, as you say, other food would affect you unfavorably?"

"Of course. Thank you."

"Anything you wish, milady." He bows and turns to the door where seven maidservants are waiting dutifully, head bowed.

He claps his hands and addresses the girls authoritatively. "This will be your new mistress, Esther from Shushan."

They line up before me and curtsy, still keeping their eyes lowered.

"You may give them new names if you wish. Do with them as you please, they are to serve your every command."

"I wish for each girl to attend to me only one day, after which they can do as they please until their turn will come up again."

I am struck by how kind the Holy One, blessed be He, is being to me. He has sent me a means to keep track of the calendar. Persians may not have a seven day week, but with the appearance of each girl,

I shall be able to count the days, and I shall be reminded when it is Shabbat, the holy day of rest.

Moreover, if each girl attends to me only one day, no one will be able to see that on the seventh, I act differently.

I approach the first girl. Tall and slender, skin dark as ebony, she stands still, with quiet confidence, though her head is bowed.

"What is your name?"

"Maimuna," she says, still looking at the ground.

"You may start attending to me today."

"And what is your name?" I ask the second girl. Short and frail, olive skin, she tugs at her apron, attempting to hide the nervous twitching of her hands.

"Samanbar," she says, raising her eyes and looking straight at me.

I gasp. *Shulamit!*

I quickly recollect my composure; I must not let my emotions betray me. I feign indifference. "You may serve me tomorrow," I say coldly.

She lowers her eyes again. I feel a twinge of guilt. I can't help feeling like I have let her down, yet I cannot allow anyone to betray my secret.

I finish assigning the girls their days of duty and dismiss all but Maimuna, who follows me silently.

"You have but to call for me and I will be at your disposal," Hegai says, before bowing and taking his leave.

I give the chamber a wide sweeping look. The *bas* reliefs are distasteful to me, with their presentations of creatures part-human, part-animals. Everything I was taught to spurn. *You shall not make for yourself a sculptured image or any picture of that which is in the heavens above, or the earth below.*

My eyes fall on a painted sculpture of a regal-looking woman. Angular, chiseled features, dark eyes, dark hair, and a fair complexion. Some might say a beautiful face, but I find beauty is an inner quality that shines outward. Her chin is cocked upward in arrogance. *And where did that lead you?* How foolish and pitiful are the ways of the conceited.

"Queen Vashti, I presume?" I ask Maimuna.

"Yes, mistress. His Highness, the king, refuses to part with any memory of her, but perhaps my mistress will succeed in replacing Vashti's place in the king's heart."

Heaven spare me!

"What happened?" I ask.

"Well, His Majesty and his company got in very high spirits toward the end of the now infamous party. The princes and satraps started boasting of the beauty of the women of their own nation. The king wanted to prove his queen was indeed the prettiest of all, and sent for her to come with only her crown on her head, so that they could all appreciate her beauty."

She clears her throat. She is trying to be as delicate as possible, not to put the king in a bad light, but how can I not be revolted by his crassness and boorishness. Oh, how I miss the pure atmosphere of my own modest little home.

"The queen at first refused. She took offense that only simple servants were called to summon her, not to mention that the request was beneath her dignity. She maintained her royal stature was superior to the king's and it had to be properly demonstrated. However, when she was made to understand that the king was not going to accept a no for an answer, she proceeded to get ready…"

She looks at the face of the sculpture and shakes her head in disbelief. "I can't quite explain it, but she suddenly became furious and hysterical, and claimed her body was covered in a rash…she couldn't and wouldn't go in that state and proceeded to insult the king in the most demeaning way possible." Maimuna sighs. "That turned out to be her own undoing, because the king's advisors insisted that were he to let her live, all women would spurn their husbands, so the king had her executed."

She shrugs wryly, no love lost.

"The king regretted doing so, and so far, no one has been able to gladden his spirit. It seems, though, that Hegai believes you'll succeed; you are being shown extra favor. Is my mistress from a royal family?"

"Is it not court protocol not to question the mistress?"

"Forgive me, my mistress," Maimuna stammers, her high cheeks becoming rosy ebony. "It won't happen again."

"I believe it is also court protocol not to share the mistress's affairs, is it not? I do treasure my privacy. Can I trust you with it?" I ask gently, but firmly.

She nods, staring at the ground, abashed.

Maimuna's innocent remarks reaffirm my necessity to be on the alert at all times. There shall be no privacy at the palace. Here, they say, even the walls have eyes and ears.

*   *   *

The days drag on, and my nights drag even longer. The fine pillows are soaked with tears, as I pray I shall be able to keep my commandments faithfully, and not betray my identity.

I think back on the words I once said so forcefully: "HaShem exiled our bodies, not our souls." Oh, exile never cut this deep before! But I meant those words then, and I mean them now. More than ever.

Shulamit is waiting by my bed with a golden bowl of water. Today is her day to attend to me. I have instructed all my maids that I like to wash my hands and face as soon as I rise. None of the other maids pay any attention to how I wash my hands, being that, in their minds, there is no significance to it. But I can see in Shulamit's eyes, how she wonders at the meaning of my every move. She knows who I really am, though I pretend never to have met her before.

I ask for candles every sunset, and light them every day, but on this evening, the sixth day of the week, I shall make the blessing over them, ushering in the holy Shabbat.

It is Divine Providence that Shulamit was assigned the sixth day, for just like her name means peace, she will help me welcome the day of peace.

I close my eyes as I whisper, "Blessed are You, Father in Heaven, King of the Universe...Who has sanctified us with the Hallowed Shabbat..."

They say the gates of Heaven are always open, but there are especially auspicious moments, as after lighting candles and ushering in the Shabbat, when the King of all Kings will welcome and accept all prayers.

I pour out my heart, praying that I should overcome whatever test HaShem has in store for me, and be reunited with Pethachia.

"Amen," Shulamit whispers with a solemn expression.

Surprised, I am speechless for a moment.

She takes my hands and kisses them with fervor. "Milady, fear not, her secret is safe with me."

I stand still, unsure how to react.

"Remember Milady told me how HaShem believes in me, and if I overcome my challenge, I'll only become stronger?" Tears stream down her oval shaped face. "From that blessed day I first met her, I have prayed to HaShem every single day, to keep me strong, to protect me. Now Vashti is gone and Milady is here. I couldn't be more fortunate." She wipes a tear with the back of her hand.

"When Milady was introduced as Esther, and after Milady pretended not to remember me, I knew Milady wanted her identity to be kept a secret. Even though Hegai asked us to try to find out who Milady is, I swear my eternal devotion to Milady. Her secret will die with me! But," She lowers her eyes in shame. "Please share with me our heritage. There is so much I don't know. The more I know, the better I can help Milady keep her secret without arousing suspicion."

I lift up my eyes to HaShem. "Blessed be Your Name, for You are good, and Your kindness is everlasting!"

I bless HaShem every day for bringing Shulamit to my aid. She is remarkably resourceful. Thanks to her, I have been able to get some kosher bread, which I enjoy, especially for the Shabbat. Not only that, but she has pointed out the other Jewish maidservants, who have sworn their allegiance to me and pledged their silence.

Just when I am getting confident I can live here as a Jew, HaShem sends another challenge my way.

"You shall be transferred to the king's harem, under my authority, of course," Hegai announces.

"May I ask why? Have I displeased you in some way?"

"Goodness, no, of course you haven't!" he exclaims. "But it's been a few months now and the King has not asked for you yet. I believe in the harem, you'll stick out like a rose among weeds, and the king will be sure to hear about you."

I do not share his enthusiasm nor his optimism.

I am again led through gardens and courtyards and more chambers, but their impressive beauty fails to enchant me, as I wonder how I will maintain my steadfast commitment in this new environment.

Thankfully, I still have my faithful maidservants by my side.

"Here we are!" Hegai says, escorting me into a large chamber, not quite as ornate as the previous lodging, but lavish nonetheless. It is swarming with women, many of them near to being undressed, reeking of a mix of sweet and pungent perfumes. Jasmine, lavender, myrrh, and goodness-knows-what-else. Some are being lathered with oils as others are bathing in steaming, petal-filled cisterns. They gabble excitedly, ordering the maids around while surveying their competition with suspicion. I feel dizzy and I stagger.

Hegai looks concerned. "Are you well, Esther? Perhaps you ought to eat more substantial food?"

"I thank you, Hegai, for your concern, but I am well. I just need to get accustomed to the smells."

Hegai smiles. "And what spice will *you* prefer?"

"None."

Hegai scratches his head. "But—"

"Do I have a displeasing odor?"

"No, but—"

"I am so grateful to you, Hegai, for making sure I am treated to the best the palace has to offer. You are doing your job excellently, the king should be pleased."

"Perhaps," says Hegai. "But it would be unseemly, and a great offense to the king, not to have any ointment at all! Please let me prevail upon you to accept this ointment, I believe it suits you."

He hands me an alabaster jug.

The sweet scent of myrtle oil pervades my nostrils.

I smile at the irony. Indeed, it does suit me. Like my real name, the myrtle has a pleasant fragrance, yet a bitter taste. Though I may be pleasant to all, I am left with a bitter taste in my mouth.

"If I must," I reply, resigned.

"Esther, it pains me to see you sad, but you must forget your past, for you will be queen."

My heart sinks. "What makes you say that?"

"I have seen many beautiful women, but you are unlike any of them. You are sure of where you stand and none of the luxuries of the palace have the power to corrupt you."

"Please, Milady," he pleads, his hand on his heart. He nods to Shifra, my maid in attendance for the day, a plump Jewish girl with round, deep-set eyes. "Proceed to bathe your mistress."

I hold out my hand to stop Shifra. "Forgive me, Hegai. If it does not importune you, and if I have found favor in your eyes, allow me to preserve my dignity in the presence of a man."

He chuckles dryly. "Everyone knows no man is allowed in the king's harem. There is no cause for concern, Esther."

I raise my eyes to meet Hegai's, though I usually refrain from looking into another man's eyes, if only to restore the dignity he was robbed of.

"Surely, you speak in jest…" The words die on his self-deprecating smile as it dawns on him that I am in earnest. He looks away, blinking. "Very well, I shall leave then," he says, clearing his throat. He bows, and proceeds to walk away, completely unaffected by the scantily clad women.

Shifra and I weave our way through the throng of women. Some are fair, some dark, some black as carbon. Some look too young to be here, some more mature, all hoping to find favor with the king. The scene before me, with all its meanings and undertones, nauseates me. I find myself a quiet corner, and Shifra starts undoing my braids and combing my hair. I pray that I find favor with the King of all Kings, that I may be free of this crass place.

"Was there nothing left in the king's treasures for you to take?" A stridulant, abrasive voice jolts me out of my misery.

A pretty woman purses her full, sensual lips while eying me suspiciously.

"So you know something we don't? What, you want me to believe you are not trying to be queen?" she jeers, congratulating herself for her perceived ironic humor.

Even if I attempt to explain that my heart belongs to another man and I yearn to be reunited with him, I doubt she will understand.

I shrug my shoulders, but she persists, annoyed at my calmness.

"You want to stand out as different? So the king will hear of you? Ah, you fool! You think that will make you queen? You know, not accepting gifts makes you a candidate for death!"

"I believe Hegai, the man in charge, has the say in the matter," I reply quietly.

"Hegai? Man?" she scoffs. "He's not a man, he's a eunuch."

"Is a bird not a bird because it lacks its wings?"

Grooves form on her forehead in her effort to process my words. She gives up and with an indignant

"Hah!", she flares her lustrous, wavy black hair, and struts away, glowering.

The truth is that in the few seconds of our interchange, her allure and beauty fast dissipated.

*   *   *

I stand in the garden, surrounded by trees bearing luscious fruit and exotic birds, but all I can see is a dark abyss opening before me. Tonight, I shall be called to the king. How I wish that I could get one more glimpse of Pethachia! I need him to strengthen me, encourage me, as he has, this past year and months since I have been taken to the palace. Notwithstanding his stature and reputation as a Jewish sage, he has walked by the harem every single day, I found out, just for the chance to catch a piece of information about my welfare. Not caring what it would look like to a stranger, or to the Jewish community, because except a handful of people, no one knows I am here.

Just knowing he is there every day, without fail, outside the harem's courtyard, fills my heart with renewed spirit. And I dare hope I will be set free, and be reunited with him. But today, all I feel is dread. I know this must be all part of HaShem's plan, but I cannot help but feel abandoned. Every limb of my body screams in protest. Cold sweat trickles down my neck.

"Milady, almond flowers, freshly picked to grace your beautiful face." An old, wizened servant lady bows and offers me the delicate pink and white blossoms. "They've come in early this winter," she says, smiling.

"Thank you, Aimai. It is very sweet of you."

"May you find favor with the king, milady," she wishes me in earnest.

I used to flinch when hearing their well-intentioned wishes, what to me sounded like curses. But I have replaced their king with HaShem, who, after all, is the King of all Kings, so that their wishes actually sound now like blessings, and I can accept them graciously.

Hegai is hovering over me like a mother hen over her eggs. He is anxiously making sure I have all I need to present myself to the king. I must admit I have not been too obliging. I am wearing a plain white tunic, a gold necklace, and a garland of ornate golden flowers Hegai has prevailed upon me to wear.

With my heart palpitating in my throat and whirling misery in the pit of my stomach, I am being led to the king's private chambers, which no one may enter, on penalty of death, but with the explicit invitation of the king.

As in a fog, I hear the chamberlain introduce me to the king, and then the gates of hell open before me.

CHAPTER FOUR

And she won grace and favor before him [the king]

(Esther 2:17)

The king's chamber is vast and dim. All around the room, tall candles burn. A deafening stillness reigns, one that is broken only by the occasional sputtering of a dying flame. I stand immobilized, shivering. I don't know whether it is from the chill of winter or the gelid wall that has besieged my heart.

"Other women have asked for the finest musicians to play and entertain, or have accepted far better gifts than you apparently have." King

Achashverosh's raspy basso booms throughout the chamber.

I am not other women.

A dark shadow emerges. Corpulent, with aquiline features, long, shaggy hair, and a dark bushy beard, Achashverosh resembles a bear more than a man.

"Tell me," he growls. "Why do you wish to be queen, have you not heard what happened to Vashti?"

"I do not wish to—" I catch my breath. I must remain calm and choose my words carefully. "I do not wish for anything other than what my king desires."

"Even if you were not chosen?" he asks, circling me like a tiger surveying its prey.

"I trust my king's judgment to be fair and true."

"Do you think what happened to Vashti was fair?"

"I believe the king ought to surround himself with wiser counselors."

"Where do you suppose I would find said advisors?"

"I am only a humble woman, but it seems to me that if something worked in the past, it should set a precedent for a positive outcome in the future."

"You speak in riddles woman, explain what you mean."

"The great leaders of the past, like Nebuchadnezzar, benefited greatly, so I have heard, from Jewish wise men. Perhaps his majesty should seek out Jewish wise men and employ them in his service."

He shifts uneasily. "I don't know about the Jews. How can one be sure they will not stab me in the back?"

My pulse quickens in indignation. How dare he! We Jews have been loyal subjects, despite his unfair treatment and higher taxes.

"The Jewish sages have been very valuable in the past. I think the wisdom of the king lies in discerning which counsel he deems appropriate to accept or reject. To discern when the counsel is being given for the benefit of the kingdom or for selfish purposes."

"True, true," he concedes.

Ah, the joys of small victories, to be able to veil insults in what he perceives as compliments.

He is intrigued and amused. He draws closer, my heart starts galloping, blood pumps in my temples, and my breathing becomes labored.

"I have heard many good things about you; all my servants seem enamored of you."

"I am fortunate to have their esteem."

Achashverosh is tickled by my response. "Modest, and humble, too, apparently," he muses. "Who are you? Where are you from?"

I can smell his wine-rancid breath. "I'm Es- Esther, from Shushan," I swallow hard.

I can feel his eyes boring into me and I have a sudden urge to vomit.

"From now on, you shall be Queen Esther, for you have charmed me and captured my heart. You shall be queen of my heart and of my kingdom!" he declares, his eyes deepening with lust.

I turn inward, letting the drumming of my heart become my focus. I want everything to go dark and clouded, wishing this nightmare to end quickly.

*   *   *

It is morning and servants come to escort me away. I am spent and numb, my eyes swollen from crying all night. Achashverosh still snores blissfully. *Why is the path of the wicked peaceful, oh, HaShem?* I shall never stop asking.

The ensuing days pass in a flurry of activity. All of Vashti's mosaic portraits are replaced by new ones of me, the artists painstakingly bringing together the glazed colored tiles on the walls. I am to choose more maidservants to attend to me. I pick Shulamit to be by my side every day, while I let the others rotate on a seven day basis, as before.

Now that the king's attentions are focused on me, I need to be even more careful not to slip. He is employing all the tactics he knows to bring me to reveal to him who I am, but I shall not falter.

"The king wishes to have your company for breakfast," the chamberlain says, bowing, his nose almost touching the ground.

I am escorted to a lovely garden. Though most trees are barren, and the air is chilled, the king is comfortably seated on a golden divan, one of a pair, under a canopy of blue and green, silver cords coiling down the columns. A lively fire is crackling in a stone basin on the outer side of each divan. Achashverosh's beady eyes light up when he sees me.

"Welcome, my queen. I have so much in store for you!" he exclaims. "We need to have a grand celebration to honor you. Let all my provinces know I have found a beautiful queen."

Shivers run through me at the thought of what happened the last time Achashverosh celebrated the beauty of his queen.

"Perhaps there is a better way to have the people celebrate."

"How so?"

"Call for a national holiday in honor of the king choosing a queen. That way, even the poor in your Kingdom will be able to truly celebrate."

"What do you mean?"

"Well, one cannot come to the palace wearing plain clothing. Suitable attire is costly."

"By Mithras, what a marvelous, generous heart you have! I'll do better. I shall send each one a gift in your honor and cut taxes for all people!"

"Your highness is very generous, but how will the Kingdom be sustained without taxes coming in?"

"My dearest, you cannot begin to imagine my wealth, if you ask such a question!" he burps complacently. "In any case, I will tax the Jews doubly," he adds, shrugging nonchalantly.

"If only I knew who your people were," he insists, while cheerfully digging his teeth into a roasted fowl. "I could show you how even more generous I can be."

"Truly, Your Majesty, I am speechless."

I clutch my cloak tight against the frosty wind of the night, as I stand between the imposing columns of the *Apadna*, the reception hall, facing lovely orchards. I watch the pale moon peek between the rolling black clouds, radiant in those few moments it owns the dark sky. I am waiting for Shulamit and Shifra to escort me to my chambers. I am exhausted. I wish I could just sleep, and wake up to a different reality.

The feast celebrated in my honor lasted for days. Through it all, I had to smile and sit by Achashverosh. He watched my every expression and nuance of movement, hoping to glean some clue about my identity. Most likely, he assumed the people would give me away, but thankfully, there are the likes of Nashiram in every nation, all adamantly convinced I am one of their own. It did not hurt that I am proficient in several languages, a gift I acquired from Mordechai, who is an accomplished linguist himself.

Mordechai. This is how I must regard him as long as I live in the palace. Mordechai, the statesman,

Mordechai as he is known among Persians, not Pethachia, *my* Pethachia.

Achashverosh even appointed Mordechai as royal advisor and judge of the King's Gate, in an effort to please me, as I had recommended him, in the hopes that I would return the favor and please him by revealing what his heart aches to know.

As I watch the moon, a wave of nostalgia overtakes me, and a tear finds its way down a familiar path. I can hear Mordechai and his colleagues chant the sanctification of the moon. *"Just as I leap toward you but cannot touch you, so may all my enemies be unable to touch me harmfully..."* The words take a poignant meaning as I pray I shall be spared further attention from Achashverosh. I am frankly mystified as to why the king should find me so endearing, when I loathe his very presence. Does he not realize how miserable I am in his company? Could he be so self-absorbed as not to notice it? Clearly, there is the Hand of HaShem in all of this, for it is nothing short of a miracle the king still desires me.

A deep, guttural voice interrupts my reverie. "Her Majesty is beautiful like the moon." A lean, dark man approaches. He bows his head, his cone-shaped hat almost brushing me as he has drawn far closer than etiquette allows. Instinctively, I turn toward the guards standing at the gateway. *Is it me? Could I be imagining the guards purposely ignoring Haman's impudence, nay, actually enjoying it?*

"Alas, it is too bad it doesn't last, and it becomes smaller and smaller until it disappears altogether," says Haman, lowering his voice to a hiss. He smiles charmingly, revealing yellowing, crooked teeth that clash with the whiteness of his wispy, long goatee.

I had met Haman previously, and had worried that his animosity towards me was because he had found out I was a Jewess. But it turned out, he held a grudge against me because he had had designs on the queen's crown for his own daughter, which I, as it happened, had foiled.

I smile inwardly at Haman's implications. Indeed, we Jews, like the moon, may wane and almost disappear into darkness at times, but we also grow back to our full splendor. May that time come, when the moon will shine as bright as the sun.

Haman is irritated by my silence and apparent lack of alarm at his veiled threat.

"Her Majesty would be wise to remember what happened to Vashti. Her position is not as secure as Her Majesty may believe. The king has ordered girls to be gathered again, *on Mordechai's advice.*"

Thank You, HaShem, my prayer has been answered! Let the king busy himself and find a better queen than me, in the meantime, I shall have some peace.

"Is there something you want from me, Haman?"

"I want to advise Her Majesty not to meddle in the king's affairs; even a queen has to remember her place as a woman."

"You are quite audacious to tell me that."

He softens his stance. "I am just trying to look out for Her Majesty's welfare. One would think that Mordechai would show some gratitude for coming to such a position because of the queen, but his very advice is threatening that position Her Majesty now holds. If you trust Jews, all you will end up with is a knife in the back."

Blood rushes to my face in indignation, but I maintain my composure. I wonder what is keeping Shifra from joining Shulamit, ever faithfully at my side, to escort me to my chambers.

"Her Majesty is mistaken in believing her position with the king is untouchable, or that the king will acquiesce to the queen's every whim. Some people don't belong in high positions of power. Why do you sympathize with Mordechai, a Jew? Are you perhaps related?"

"One need not be related to recognize or appreciate wisdom."

"Her Highness may be well intentioned, but I happen to know Mordechai from past experiences, his charm doesn't fool me. Here is advice Her Highness would be wise to heed. Fortunes may change in a blink of an eye, and one may not have the king to rely on."

"Is that so?"

"Please accept this goodwill gesture, given with the utmost sincerity, Your Highness," he says, bowing again with exaggerated obsequiousness.

I watch him strut away, my heart palpitating, my palms sweating.

When he is out of sight, Shulamit mutters an imprecation. "How can you remain quiet while he insults you and your people? Where do you get that strength?"

"From our ancestress, Rachel."

Her eyes widen in delighted expectation, she loves to hear of our heritage.

"Pray tell, Your Majesty."

"Jacob, our forefather, loved Rachel and wished to marry her, but he knew he could not trust her father, Laban, who was sure to swindle him and perhaps sneak in a strange woman instead of the promised bride."

"But wouldn't he notice if it wasn't Rachel?"

"The custom at that time was for a bride to be veiled, and in any case, Laban was shrewd enough to come up with ways to mislead people.

"So Jacob devised a plan. He gave Rachel a secret code, only she would know the answers to the riddle he would propose to the bride under the canopy. Imagine Rachel's consternation when, right before the wedding, Leah, her dear sister, was being prepared to be married. She thought of how ashamed Leah would be when Jacob would expose her as a fraud, and she could not bear to let her sister suffer such humiliation. So she did the unthinkable; she gave Leah the secret code. She gave away her chance to be with the man she loved."

"But didn't Jacob marry her, too?"

"Yes, later, but Rachel had no way of knowing that. She assumed Jacob would hate her for her betrayal, but Jacob appreciated the sacrifice Rachel had made for her sister, and only loved her the more for it. So he married Rachel, too, and worked another seven years for her, even though it was very uncommon to marry sisters."

"So how do you learn the power of silence from her?"

"Just from reading the text of the Torah, you would never know Rachel did that, and it is never brought up at any time thereafter. We only know of it because it has been passed down from generation to generation. Rachel kept silent when she realized Leah was being given as a bride and never mentioned her sacrifice thereafter."

King Shaul, too, I muse to myself. *Had inherited that quality.* He was chosen as the first king in Israel, yet he kept quiet about the matter until he was forced into it. A sudden vision of the tall, noble man from my dream flashes into my mind. I see the intensity of his eyes, eyes just like mine. All at once, like a bolt of lightning across a dark sky, I am certain the man in the dream is my ancestor King Shaul. We are connected by something far deeper than blood, and my being here at the palace is part of that connection. How? I do not yet understand.

CHAPTER FIVE

When Mordechai was sitting in the King's Gate. .

(Esther 2:21)

The encounter with Haman left me in a state of heightened alarm. Though I only met him at the palace, I am acquainted with his history through Mordechai's dealings with him. They go back several years.

Early on, in the second year of Achashverosh's reign, Mordechai and Haman were assigned to quell a rebellion in Hindika, an Indian province. Each was allocated six thousand troops and provisions for three years. Mordechai led his men on the offense to the east, Haman to the west. Haman squandered his provisions within the first year, running out of supplies. He went to Mordechai and asked for help, but Mordechai had to refuse him. He could not trust Haman to use the supplies wisely, and not knowing how long the campaign was going to last, he had to think about his own troops. Haman returned to his men empty-handed, only to return to Mordechai a short while later, pleading for his life. His men, hungry and tired of his hollow promises, were threatening a mutiny. Mordechai agreed only on the condition that Haman would become his servant. That way, Mordechai would be in charge of all the decisions, and outwardly, Haman would still appear to have authority over his troops. Haman agreed and a contract was drawn up on Mordechai's greave.

Before long, under Mordechai's skilled leadership, the campaign came to a successful end. One would think that Haman would have felt gratitude toward Mordechai for having saved his life and his honor, as the contract was kept private. Instead, it only served to augment his hate for Mordechai, the Jew. I suppose that for someone who nursed such a visceral hate for Jews, one inherited from his ancestors the Amalekites, to be indebted to a Jew must have been particularly infuriating.

"The king wishes to have your company, Your Highness," Maimuna announces, breaking my chain of thought.

I flinch. A tempest of emotions swirls into a cyclone: anger, contempt, self-pity, misery. I want to scream or break something. *What is happening to me? Why am I feeling this way, where is my faith? Am I going crazy?*

My head starts spinning and my legs give way. Maimuna and Shulamit rush to support me, and lay me gently on the bed.

"I'll let the chamberlain know you will need a moment," says Maimuna, pursing her thick lips.

I had hoped that if I escaped the nights, as the king was otherwise entertained, I would also be spared during the day. Alas, this was not to be.

"Does the king have no other duties to attend to?" I lament, dolefully massaging my temples.

"The king loves you," says Maimuna, softly.

An exasperated sneer escapes me. Achashverosh is incapable of love. I cry tears of misery and he mistakes them for elation. All he is capable of is indulging himself.

"Perhaps the queen ought to see the healer. Her Majesty does seem pale," ventures Maimuna, surprised at my uncharacteristic outburst.

"It's alright," I reassure her with a faint smile. "It is as you said, I just need a few more moments to collect myself."

We make our way through the idol-infested courtyards, our steps echoing in the vast and silent halls. The bulls perched atop the columns glitter in the sunlight. I cringe at their sight.

I shall never get used to this.

Though I have passed these halls countless times, the offending images never become familiar to me. And so it should be. Woe to me, were I to become numb to all of this. It would be the day I lost touch with who I really am, and that can never be.

A knot forms in my throat and I have trouble swallowing.

Do not cry, not now.

Why am I feeling such despair? Where is my faith in the All-knowing, All-merciful HaShem?

I cannot fathom His reasons, but His thoughts are not like ours. I may not understand, but HaShem saw fit to put me here, undoubtedly for a good and just purpose. I believe that, and Mordechai believes that, too. I must be strong.

The guard at the gate of the king's private chamber nods and grunts as he allows me access to the chamber. He seems angry for some reason. I give him a sympathetic look, but I am wholly unprepared for his reaction. Daggers of hate shoot from his eyes and I recoil in surprise.

I ought to mentally prepare myself to resist Achashverosh's manipulations. He is as adamant as ever to discover my background and identity. Yet I cannot help but strain my brain, endeavoring to recall what I might have done to cause that guard to hate me so. He did look somewhat familiar.

"Do you know that guard?" I whisper to Shulamit.

"Yes, that's Bigthan, a distant cousin of Vashti. Your Majesty ought to be wary of him, for he resents you."

Suddenly, it dawns on me where I had seen him before: smirking devilishly when Haman had accosted me.

The thought of the two of them conspiring alarms me. I must alert Mordechai.

*   *   *

I walk with resolute steps, unconcerned at some raised eyebrows that meet me. True, royal women are not commonly seen in these parts of the palace, but it is not unheard of either. As I near the King's Gate, I suppress the smile that is bursting on my lips. The thought of seeing Mordechai still makes my heart exult like a young bride. It is a glimmer of light in the midst of abject darkness, a breath of fresh air in a suffocating environment.

Mordechai approaches me and bows. "Blessing unto you, Your Highness," he proclaims loudly. "We need to talk," he whispers as he bows.

"I came to observe you, Mordechai. Praise of your wisdom has reached me and I wished to see it for myself," I assert with an authoritative tone. "Would you be so kind to accompany me back to the gardens, I wish you to solve some riddles that have eluded me for a while."

"I will try my best, Your Highness," Mordechai obliges.

We stroll down the vineyards, closely followed by my trusted maidservants. We whisper like conspirators while maintaining a detached appearance.

"Are you all right, Esther? I hear you've had fainting spells. Are you eating enough?"

"How did you find out?" I do not want Mordechai to worry about me. His time is too precious, the Jewish community needs him.

He smiles. "You cannot imagine how much gossip one can hear, just sitting by the Gate."

His flowing white beard sways gently as he talks and I find myself reveling in the memories of his sweet, good face. *How I miss him. Is it my imagination or has the line on his forehead deepened?*

"Your Highness?"

"Yes," I reply, startled. "Please, carry on..."

Mordechai's eyes narrow. "It is good you came, otherwise, I would have found you. There is an extremely important matter I have to disclose to you," he says, lowering his voice to a whisper.

I nod gravely.

"There is a plot to assassinate the king by his personal guards, Bigthan and Theresh."

"I thought they were conspiring with Haman. How have you come upon this knowledge?"

"They were talking in Tarsyan, sure that no one could understand them. Apparently, they hold a few grudges against the king, and they plan to place a poisonous snake in the water decanter. Being that they often have to bring water to the king in the middle of the night..." His voice trails off, deep lines furrowing his brow. "You must let the king know."

"Perhaps, you should go tell the king, you will gain favor in his eyes that way."

"No, you are right to think that Haman may be involved. Who knows who else is conspiring with them? I'm afraid they will not allow me access to the king or they will twist my words and turn the facts against me. You should do it, and gain the king's favor. I know he pesters you on account of your mysterious identity, and he is suspicious of everyone. This will prove to him that you are loyal."

"If you think this is best."

"Be careful."

I nod. A sinking feeling intensifies as I know our time must end.

I raise my head, forcing a smile. "Thank you for your wisdom, it has been a very pleasant chat," I state with dry decorum.

Then Mordechai hands me, surreptitiously, a small rolled papyrus. My inquisitive, surprised look is met by a twinkle in his eyes. A warm sensation spreads down my chest as I understand.

"You have given me life," I whisper as I clutch the precious gift. "It means everything to me."

"I know," he says, smiling somberly.

It is comforting to know there is one person in the world who knows and appreciates me for who I truly am in every aspect. I hold the Torah Syllabus close to my heart, knowing it will bring me solace in my darkest hours.

He bows and turns to leave.

My heart grows heavier as I watch his figure shrink in the distance.

*   *   *

Achashverosh slams the rython on the table, the wine spilling over the golden lion-head of the rython.

"Dearest queen," he growls. "You seem distracted today." There is a hint of annoyance in Achashverosh's voice.

I have been deliberately ignoring him, partly to gain his attention, and partly because I am trying to figure out the best course of action. Bigthan and Theresh are not to be underestimated. They enjoy the king's trust as they have been his personal guards for many years. If I am going to accuse them, I must ascertain that the evidence of their murderous plot is not cleverly discarded.

"Forgive me, Your Majesty, I am distraught…for good reason."

"What is it?"

"Rumors of an attempt at His Majesty's life, from subjects who enjoy the king's utmost trust."

Achashverosh's flat forehead furrows. His small beady eyes darken. "What do you know? What have you heard?" he says, leaning his corpulent neck forward.

"I believe it imperative for the perpetrators to be caught in the act. Only then will the king have certainty."

"What do you propose?" he bleats, wringing his big hands together.

"Next time His Majesty requests a drink or a meal, right before taking it, His Majesty should offer it to the one who has prepared it for the king. Whatever the reaction, the king will know how to proceed."

"Yes…yes," he grumbles pensively, sitting back on his couch, somewhat relieved. "I will know what to do." He drums the tips of his finger together, lost in morose thoughts.

*　　*　　*

Only two days later, Bigthan and Theresh were indeed arrested, and the investigation corroborated what Mordechai had told me. A poisonous snake was found in the water decanter where water is kept for the king's use, and neither could explain the reason for their absences. They were executed by impalement for high treason. Unfortunately, Haman managed to escape scrutiny. I would not be surprised if, with time, he were going to take credit for thwarting the plot. Considering that the king's personal scribe is Haman's son, Shimshi, I insisted on overseeing the recording of this event in the king's personal chronicle book and I made sure that Mordechai was given the credit due to him.

Sometimes I wonder what would have been if Mordechai had not overheard the plot, and therefore felt compelled to intervene. What if Achashverosh *had* been killed? What would have happened to me then? Would I have been able to go back to Mordechai? I admit it is silly to play these mind games, "what if". One needs to live with what is, and make the best of it.

*   *   *

A fit of dizziness and nausea overtakes me, and I find myself kneeling and vomiting on the fine studded carpet. Shulamit and Shifra come to my aid.

"Your Majesty, please let me call the healer this time," Shulamit pleads, her pointy chin quivering.

"No, No, I am fine," I insist feebly. I do not want the healer to compel me to eat non-kosher meat. When the great sages Daniel, Hananiah, Mishael, and Azariah refused to eat King Nebuchadnezzar's food, HaShem made them healthier than the rest of the courtiers. Much like me, they were forcibly taken from their homes to serve the king. They were young, but resolute to keep their faith at all costs. I, too, shall keep strong and be strengthened by refusing to eat the king's non-kosher food.

Shifra eyes me knowingly. "Indeed, Your Majesty does not need a healer," she says smiling.

I look at her questioningly.

"Your Highness," she says sweetly, dabbing a wet cloth on my face. "I believe you are with child."

CHAPTER SIX

After these events...(Esther 3:1) *G-d prepares the remedy before the affliction (rashi)*

I pick an apricot off a tree, its fuzzy exterior tickling my fingers.

I close my eyes and take a deep breath. The sweet aroma of ripened fruit invades my lungs, the golden morning rays caress my skin, and for a moment, surrounded by HaShem's nature, I am lost in a timeless space. Whispering trees, gurgling waters, the humming of winged little creatures; I savor this music, this fleeting taste of freedom. Indeed, the *Bisan*, the king's magnificent garden, is where I come when I need to clear my mind. Here, my prison walls relent, and my lips whisper the words of King David. They flow effortlessly, by memory, drawing me into a sense of solace and purpose.

Trust in HaShem...and He will grant you the desires of your heart...depend on HaShem and hope in Him...let go of anger, abandon rage...for soon the wicked one will not be; you will gaze at his place and he will be gone...the steps of man are directed by HaShem for he desires His way.

For He desires His way. Then who am I to say I desire differently? True, the news struck me like lightning in the midst of a placid summer sky. Me? Expecting a child? How could it be? Years of fervent prayers, married to a saintly man, and I was not deserving of a child. One night with a hedonistic, self-centered, tyrannical heathen, and I am expecting? But if this is what HaShem desires, then who am I to spurn the soul that is growing within me?

*   *   *

The large, embroidered traveling tents have already set into motion, embarking on a month-long journey to Parsa. The king's enormous tent is aptly named "the movable palace". In it, over two hundred of the "closest" relatives attend to the king, followed by thirty thousand foot soldiers and hundreds of royal horses. Soon after, albeit with more difficulty, there follow a dozen *harmamaxae*, wagons in which the king's children and their governesses ride. Eunuchs accompany them, together with a glittering, colorful mass of concubines, all regally dressed and adorned. Competing with their shrill boisterousness, six hundred mules and three hundred camels trail behind, carrying the king's money. A guard of bowmen follows closely. Soon, in a less orderly manner, they will be joined by the king's relatives and friends, along with caterers, wine-clarifiers, perfume-makers, and servants, lest the basic essentials the king cannot do without might be overlooked. Lightly-armed men and their officers will bring up the rear of the procession. Along the journey, the entire entourage will leave behind fields scattered with the king's riches, treasures for anyone to plunder to his heart's content.

Achashverosh, mounted on his gray horse, approaches. Both are adorned so extravagantly, it would humble peacocks.

"Are you certain, my beloved, that you wish to remain in Shushan for the summer?" he asks, one last attempt to convince me to join his entourage. "It does get unbearably hot."

"His Majesty need not worry on my account, I shall be provided for. I fear the trip might compromise the health of the unborn child."

"May Arumazda find you deserving and reward you with a son."

I wince.

Save your inept gods for yourself.

"Let your heart not be troubled, my queen. Even if your beauty should lessen, you'll always be queen of my heart."

Is that what worries him? It dawns on me that perhaps that is why I am not summoned at night. Does this mean I no longer have to fear that he might? Blessed is His Name forever for making Achashverosh so shallow.

Tears find their way out, of their own volition.

"Do not be distressed, my dearest," Achashverosh says. "You know I only desire your happiness." He motions to the young servant holding the golden stool and dismounts his horse with a bit of difficulty, laden as he is with the royal attire. "If only I knew who your family was, I would raise them to the highest offices and then I am certain you would be the happiest woman in the world!"

"Your Majesty is too kind. I do not deserve the esteem you so generously afford me."

Achashverosh is moved by my flattery. Though he is adulated all day long by his subjects, he craves, more than anything else, recognition by a peer. Inwardly, he nurses a feeling of inferiority because of his mother's low status as a concubine. Vashti rarely accorded him the respect due his stature, and never lost an opportunity to vaunt her superiority. Although he appreciated her political acumen, he resented that she constantly reaffirmed his deep insecurities. That is why he insists in his quest to find out who I am and where I come from. He hopes I prove to be his equal in aristocracy, yet I remain a mystery to him. He suspects I am from regal stock. Indeed I am, but he cannot fathom why I would feel shame to reveal it, for what else could possibly prevent me from doing so? I am surprised he has not thought of the Jewish connection. Could he be so prejudiced against the Jews, he cannot fathom one of them beautiful?

"My queen, my love for you is such that I am promoting Haman, the one responsible for your appointment as queen, to become one of my personal advisors, an honor that is usually reserved only for the Persian nobility."

I am stunned beyond words, but Achashverosh is too preoccupied congratulating himself for his magnanimous generosity to notice I am other than pleased.

"And I am putting at your personal disposition, Hathach!" he says, pointing toward the King's Gate where shortly before, servants were sent scurrying to summon Hathach, or as I knew him, Daniel.

The great Daniel, whom Nebuchadnezzar took together with the best of the Jewish nobility, to serve him. Whom HaShem had endowed with the gift of wisdom, who predicted and foresaw Nebuchadnezzar's downfall, who came unscathed out of the lions' den, where King Darius had thrown him.

I stand mesmerized, watching the aged yet proud and noble figure advance toward us.

"It will be my honor and privilege to serve the queen," says Daniel in his soft wispy voice, bowing his head in reverence.

"Very well then," says Achashverosh, mounting back on his horse. "I shall see you in the fall."

With a brusque tug at the reins, he turns his steed, spurs the horse into a trot, and joins his traveling tents.

Horns blast in the distance, heralding the start of the regal procession.

My heart is full at the unexpected gift HaShem has brought my way. I have had conflicted emotions about this pregnancy and misgivings about discussing it with Mordechai, but now who better to assuage my fears than Daniel, who has lived at the royal court for nearly a century and kept his faith strong?

"Will you kindly escort me to the *Bisan*? There is much I'd like to talk about."

"Certainly, Your Highness."

We stroll in silence, absorbed in our thoughts. Daniel's steps are deliberate and resolute. There is a vigor about him that is surprising for a person his age. His posture is erect and his face is strong but kind, his demeanor comforting. I feel safe in his presence.

"Forgive me for asking," I venture. "But what have you done to incur Achashverosh's displeasure?"

"What do you mean?"

"You are a legend at Court, you have been the previous kings' right hand man and now you have been demoted to look after the queen?"

"Serving you, Your Highness, is not a demotion, rather an advancement," he says buoyantly.

"Do not misunderstand me; I believe the Merciful Father in Heaven has brought you to me for

I dearly need your counsel, but what is Achashverosh's excuse?"

"You are quite right, I have incurred Achashverosh's displeasure by suggesting one time too many he should allow for the Jews to rebuild the holy Beit Hamikdash."

"Jeremiah's prophecy…" I whisper.

"Oh, yes, I had hoped that the seventy years would have started from when Nebuchadnezzar exiled us, but alas, I am afraid it will be seventy years from the destruction of our holy Temple."

"But that is not for another decade!" I exclaim.

An eternity.

"You think I might be able to influence him?"

"No," he replies somberly. "I do not believe it possible."

"Why?" I ask. "Is it fear or hatred, for Jews? I cannot comprehend it. His predecessors did not have such fixations. They allowed all religions their liberty. Cyrus permitted the rebuilding of the Beit

Hamikdash, until some libelous tongues caused him to rescind."

Daniel strokes his snowy white beard pensively. "I think he believes letting the Jews rebuild the Beit Hamikdash would mean relinquishing control or power over them, and while his predecessors attributed their sovereignty to divine power, Achashverosh gives credit to himself alone. You see, his father, King Darius, had older sons from his queen to take over his reign, but Achashverosh prevailed upon Darius to bequeath the throne to him instead."

"He does seem to have a constant need to prove to the world his legitimacy." I mutter to myself.

"Rumors have it that it was reported to Achashverosh that the stars predicted that a Jew would take his crown, so he fears that, too."

Instinctively I bring my hand over my belly.

"My child…" I murmur with a sudden realization. "He will succeed him."

Tears spring out of my eyes.

"How could I have a child here?" I cry. "For years, I begged HaShem for a child, and I imagined I would have to suffer like our matriarch, Rachel, but this is not how I wanted it. How can I possibly raise this child as a Jew in this accursed place?"

"It is not in our hands, Esther." he says, empathy radiating out of every wrinkle. "HaShem has His reasons. And perhaps this child will be the one to fulfill the prophecy."

His kind and penetrating gaze warms me, yet he seems to be looking past me, into some distant future.

"Be strong, Esther, and be strengthened. Salvation will come through you and the baby you are carrying."

"Amen." I whisper, wiping away my tears, a new sense of purpose anchoring me.

"Will you teach him and guide him?"

"I will personally see to it that he is provided with the best instructors."

"Thank you."

"However," he says gravely, suddenly looking tired. "You will have to be on guard even more carefully from now on, as I have heard that Haman shall be promoted. He will work to undermine whatever influence you exert on the king. There is no more skillful slanderer in the world than Haman."

I nod, steeling myself for the hardship to come.

"May HaShem guard you and protect you."

CHAPTER SEVEN

But Mordechai would neither kneel nor prostrate himself

[before Haman]

(Esther 3:2)

Five years have passed, and Daniel's words of caution regarding Haman's appointment have proved prophetic. Notwithstanding Achashverosh's notorious suspiciousness, Haman has successfully insinuated himself into Achashverosh's confidence, gaining the king's blind trust. From a foreign nobody, Haman has climbed his way to the top echelons. Still, that has not stopped the Persian and Median aristocracy from snubbing him. In retaliation, Haman induced Achashverosh to make a decree that even nobles are to prostrate to him, though that is expected only of commoners. Haman cunningly claimed that the decree was a necessity to discern true loyalty among the nobles. Were they to disrespect Haman because of his less-than-pure background, would that not be implying that Achashverosh, just like Haman, was not legitimate? Indeed, Haman plays on the king's deep-seated insecurities, as a virtuoso would a harp.

I walk past the *Apadna* to my favorite spot of the *Bisan*, the magnificent royal garden. Here is where I come to gather my thoughts, to meet with my allies and strategize how to safeguard my secret and ensure my survival at court. Here is where a cluster of cedar trees stand tall and have grown taller each year since my son's first birthday. It is hard to believe that four years have passed so quickly. It seems like it was just the other day, when my son was born to me, and I suggested cedar trees be brought from west of the Euphrates to plant in the *Bisan* with the wish that the Crown Prince would grow strong and tall like the cedar trees. I whisper my wish, expressed so eloquently by King David.

The righteous will grow tall like a cedar, planted in the House of HaShem, they shall blossom and be fruitful even in old age; they shall be full of sap and freshness—to declare HaShem is just.

The sun, perched high in the morning sky, is particularly scalding this early in the spring, but in the shade of the cedar trees, there is a pleasant breeze, the green branches softly swaying in a slow, alluring dance.

A group of gardeners are hard at work nearby, digging, their once white tunics brown with dirt.

I approach them. "Good day to you, what are you working on?" I smile.

Flustered, the workers turn to me and kneel. "Forgive us, Your Highness, for our improper attire. Please accept our humble greetings," they bleat, wiping the freshly dug earth off their hands on their aprons.

"Please, do not let my presence interrupt your work. Are you planting something?"

"Yes, Your Highness, we are planting new lilies so that Your Ladyship may enjoy them in a couple of months."

"I am delighted to hear that. I do appreciate their delicate elegance."

"Your Highness' grace is immeasurable." They bow, their faces touching the ground.

I nod courteously. Most people mean well, but within the palace walls, not all smiles are sincere. Many hide poison behind their honeyed façade. One cannot afford to be naïve, if one is to survive unscathed.

Before Darius was born, time was at a standstill, unbearably so, but ever since his birth, my days have been filled with purpose. I have something to live for now, to ensure my son's safety so that he may yet fulfill his destiny. He is only four and a half years old but his enemies within the palace's walls abound. Concubines who have born sons wish to get rid of

Darius to give their sons a chance to inherit the throne. Haman and his accomplices see him as a hindrance to their rise to power because of my influence on him.

I pace restlessly, waiting. I've sent for Nechemia, a great scholar in the Jewish community, a colleague of Ezra and Mordechai, and a welcomed addition to palace life.

I dig my leather slippers into the ground, treading soft pink almond blossoms that have carpeted the garden.

Where could he be?

I assume he is going to come from the King's Gate. I shield my eyes from the sun with my hand, searching the eastern horizon.

Finally, I spot Nechemia approaching from the distance. The familiar lopsided gait, the tunic loose-hanging on his slight frame, the absorbed expression on his face, brings a smile to my lips. I wish there were more of his caliber effecting influence on my son, Darius. Nechemia is erudite in Torah but knowledgeable in the ways of Persian society as well; he can masterfully weave his way through palace politics as well as extricating laws from our sacred writings.

Nechemia bows. "Blessing unto you, Your Majesty." His melodious voice sounds like a song whenever he talks.

"I'd like to hear the latest report on Prince Darius' progress. Why is he spending less time with you and more with Baratkama? Under whose order was that change implemented?"

"Your Majesty knows very well that a Persian's priorities are to ride a horse, draw a bow, and speak the truth. I can only help him with the last one, and I have been bidden by the king to allow the Crown Prince to acquire and perfect the other skills."

"I see."

Of course, out of the three priorities, the last one seems to fall by the wayside. I dare say that is why they drink in excess, to be able to speak the truth.

Though my son is remarkably precocious and displays a maturity beyond his tender four and a half years, he is still impressionable. I have made it my business to direct the influences on him as much as possible, so I am pleased that Darius has formed an attachment to Nechemia.

"It is very important to me that you continue to instruct the Crown Prince as before."

"Yes, Your Royal Highness," he says, bowing.

"If I may, Your Highness…" Nechemia starts, after a moment's hesitation.

"Please, speak your mind."

"I know how strongly the queen feels about having the Crown Prince attend your er…special dinner…"

It takes me a moment before I grasp Nechemia's intent. I always particularly cherished Passover, and though, with a heavy heart, I refrain from including Darius in activities that would compromise my secret identity, the Seder is something I take great pains to have Darius participate in.

"Though the Crown Prince has been 'a son who does not know what to ask', or his questions have been innocent enough for Your Highness to deflect them, I fear it won't be the case this year. Just over the last few months, the Crown Prince has shown tremendous progress in his intellectual abilities. Unless Your Highness feels the Crown Prince is ready to know…"

"No, he should not be burdened by that," I mutter, my mind feverishly looking for a possible solution. I refuse to forgo the chance for Darius to participate at a Seder. It hurts to see my Jewish child being raised as a pagan, so at least I want him to experience Passover. It holds poignant symbolic meaning as it marks when HaShem first chose us as His nation.

A flurry of colorful feathers draws our attention. A few exotic birds go squawking and scurrying off in all directions as Darius comes running wildly, cheeks aflush and eyes shining, wide with excitement.

"Baratkama took me riding today and I held the reins all by myself!" he blurts out, panting.

Stern looks from the court ladies subdue his euphoria almost instantly.

"Blessing unto you, *Duksis* Mother," he says, bowing courteously.

"Blessing unto you, dear Prince Darius. Will the Crown Prince join me for a walk?"

"Yes, *Duksis* Mother."

I turn to Nechemia. "I will take your words into consideration, but I believe there might be other solutions." An idea is starting to form in my mind, but I ought to confer with Mordechai. I know that he has dealt in the past on behalf of Jews on military posts, like the garrison in Elephantine, whom the king granted leave for *Pesach*.

"Please precede us to the King's Gate. The Crown Prince and I will join you soon. I would like for Prince Darius to practice writing on papyrus as well as on the clay tablets."

Nechemia bows and takes his leave.

The orchard this time of year is fragrant, with trees in bloom. We stroll leisurely along the endless tree rows, making small talk. Mindlessly, Darius plucks a flower and rips it into shreds.

"Was there a reason for you to destroy that flower?"

"No, why?"

"One day, you will be king and you will inherit power over many people. What are you going to do with that power?" I bend down to face him and place my hands on his shoulders. "A flower is a life, too. When you hold a life in your hand, you have a responsibility to respect it."

He nods, avoiding my gaze and biting his lips to hide a quiver.

I hug him tight, running my hand over his thick, unruly mane of dark curls. "You will make a fine king," I reassure him.

I ease my grip when I feel him relaxing. We continue our walk in silence.

"Mother?"

"Yes, Darius?"

"Did you grow up among nobles? Did your family serve them?"

I eye him warily. "Did the king put you up to this?"

"Why can you not say?"

"You need not worry about your mother's lineage. Your father became king on his father's account, not his mother's, and so will you."

"But it vexes him so that you refuse to tell him."

"I do not wish to vex him, but I cannot do it."

I resent that Achashverosh is burdening Darius with affairs that appertain to him and I alone.

"Regardless, it should not concern you; it is between the king and me."

"But it does concern me!" he protests with feeling. "Haman dislikes you and he is turning the king against you! Has not an interpreter been appointed to speak for you as if you were a mere commoner, undeserving to speak to the king directly? He never felt the need to before. How long before…" The words get stuck in his throat as he dares not say it out loud.

If only I could take away that fear and pain I see in your eyes.

A knife thrust into my heart would have been easier to bear.

What can I say that will make your worry dissipate? That there is a plan HaShem has in store for you and me, and we need only to put our trust in Him.

Darius lets out a sigh of frustration. He reaches for a tulip, but decides against it.

"Even if the queen's family were slaves, the king could make them noble, could he not? Haman would have nothing to say because he came to his position the same way." A spark of hope brightens his eyes.

I look at him in wonderment; so young and he already has such a profound understanding of the palace's workings. If only he could dive that acumen into the waters of Torah! Still, he will make a fine king.

"I promise there will come a time you will know," I say softly. "A very wise man once said there is a time for everything…"

"King Solomon."

"I see you have been instructed well."

A warm voice I know so well interjects, startling me. "Her Majesty is very fond of King Solomon's wisdom."

"Mordechai!"

We had been so absorbed in our conversation, I had not realized we had reached the King's Gate.

He bows his head. "Forgive me for intruding, Your Highness," he says. "Your arrival was announced and I wanted to pay my respects. I happened to overhear your comment. Please pardon this humble servant's impudence."

"You are forgiven," I say kindly. "It is hardly a secret I admire wisdom, wherever it is to be found."

"BOW TO HAMAN, BY ORDER OF THE KING," The screeching cry we have come to endure interrupts our pleasant moment.

As the voice of the crier blasts through the Gate, echoing in the vast chamber, Shulamit rolls her eyes. "Must he parade himself even here? Did the palace become his playground?" she mutters under her breath, gritting her teeth.

Haman, flanked by guards and servants, comes strutting by, his hook nose thrust in the air.

Darius draws closer to me. Legs spread apart, fists clenched, he narrows his eyes, staring Haman down in a defiant stance.

In the midst of a sea of prostrated forms, Mordechai stands out like a lone palm tree in the desert, his posture erect and proud.

Haman approaches. "Greetings, Your Highness," he says smiling, making a feeble attempt at being cordial. "May I ask what brings Her Majesty to the King's Gate?"

"The King's Gate is where justice is dispensed. As future king of this empire, it is never too soon to learn how to become just and wise," I say, wrapping my arm around Darius. *You will not touch him. HE will be king*

Haman suppresses a sneer. "I see. Still, Her Majesty didn't have to bother to come all the way out here," he says, shifting his gaze from me to Mordechai.

My heart skips a beat. *Is he making the connection? Was I too imprudent?*

"True, but what can I do? As a mother, I enjoy watching my son's prodigious abilities," I say as affably as I can.

"Her Majesty the queen's concern for the Crown Prince's education is commendable. I would dare to say that it is imperative for all the king's subjects to show Prince Darius their duty to the Crown, wouldn't you say, Mordechai?" he hisses, turning to face him. "Is it not treasonous to blatantly disregard the king's command?"

"What command do you speak of?" Mordechai replies calmly and earnestly.

Haman almost chokes with fury. "What command?!" he sputters. "To kneel and prostrate yourself to Haman, son of Hamedatha, the Agagite!" he roars, his veins bulging.

"Is it not also the king's command to allow all subjects the freedom to serve their gods as they please?" Mordechai replies, maintaining his calm demeanor.

"So?"

"You carry an idol around your neck. As a Jew, I only bow to the G-d of Israel."

"And if I were to take off my idol, would you then bow to me?"

"No."

"Why not?" Haman snarls, nostrils flaring.

"Because you always carry that idol with you, and I don't want anyone to assume it is alright for a Jew to bow to an idol. As a leader of the Jewish people, I ought to set an example."

"Jews have bowed down to idols before, they did under Nebuchadnezzar."

"All the more reason I should not."

"Even your ancestor, Jacob, bowed to Esau."

"I see you are familiar with our history. Then you should know that his son, Benjamin, never did bow to Esau, for he was not yet born. That merit was always a credit to him, which is why the Almighty saw fit to build the Temple in his portion of the land. As his descendant, I ought to follow his example."

"Are you not afraid of the consequences of your insubordination?"

"I am not afraid to do the right thing."

"The king does not tolerate disobedience."

"The king does not tolerate incompetence either." Mordechai intimates, subtly revealing an old greave under his long white tunic.

Haman's face becomes livid and without saying another word, he storms off, his retinue scampering behind him.

"What was that?" Darius blurts out, voicing what most people are wondering.

"Never mind that. Go along, Prince Darius, Nechemia is waiting for you to instruct you."

I wait for him to disappear into one of the chambers, then, after throwing some furtive glances around me, I turn to Mordechai. "Why did you taunt him?" I whisper, throwing a glance at his greave. I recognize it as the one in which Mordechai had written the contract, years ago, postulating that Haman was to become his servant in exchange for food and supplies.

"I wasn't taunting him, just reminding him."

"Still, it will only motivate him to rid himself of you."

"Which reminds me: I did not like the way he was looking at you and me. From now on, you need to take extra precautions to ensure he won't uncover our relation. I don't have to tell you that the palace's walls have eyes and ears."

I nod reluctantly.

A curt signal to my ladies, and we take our leave, much to my regret, as there is still so much I wish to discuss with Mordechai.

I sigh. "Samanbar, we are going to be very busy preparing our special dinner, it's only a couple of weeks away."

"Yes, Your Highness."

I wonder if this will be the first year Darius won't be attending the Seder. This event has upset me more than I care to admit. A dark and heavy feeling looms over me, one I cannot easily shake off.

It is not long before Haman confirms my foreboding. I am standing in between the towering columns of the Apadna, their marble bases so wide, a man could comfortably stretch out to sleep on them. I am marveling at how much effort it must have taken to build this palace, when Haman strides toward me with a smirk on his face. He bears the look of a lion about to pounce on his prey.

"Blessing unto you, Your Highness," he sneers. "I have come to pay homage to Her Majesty." He pauses. I brace myself for the poison that is to follow his honeyed greeting. "Was it not five years ago, shortly after Her Ladyship became queen, that we met in this very place and I gave the queen advice? Does Her Highness remember?"

How can I forget? You outright threatened me, and it was not too long after, that an attempt on the king was made. If Mordechai had not foiled your plans, would I have been next?

"I wondered then, why you showed such graciousness toward Mordechai, and petitioned the king to appoint him at the King's Gate, but now all is clear."

I inhale sharply.

"How so?" I ask innocently, smiling obligingly to hide a tremor.

"I suppose Her Ladyship feels indebted to Mordechai for having been his ward, but let me assure you, it was not done out of kindness. I know Mordechai better than anyone. He had designs for you to become queen so that he could gain power through you. Is it not so?"

My heart skips a beat. *Just how much has he found out about me and Mordechai?*

"You see, Mordechai belongs to a fringe fanatical group of Jews who believe they ought to go back to Jerusalem and rebuild their sacred temple. They succeeded in convincing King Cyrus, but thankfully, I was able to halt the construction. Their true aim is to overthrow the king and become all powerful like they were in the times of Solomon."

Are you not revealing your own heart and designs, Haman?

"I am not sure I follow what you are saying."

"Perhaps Mordechai has asked you to petition the king to allow the Jews to return to their homeland and rebuild their temple. In my capacity as Viceroy, I recommend the queen avoid such political matters. The king would be displeased. Whatever debt Your Ladyship might owe Mordechai, consider it more than paid off."

"I see."

"I realize why Her Highness kept the matter a secret, that Her Ladyship was a ward of Mordechai, I would not be proud of it either." He twirls his thin mustache with his heavily ring-clad hand. "Her Highness is certainly aware of how high the king's regard for me is," he says smugly. "It would be my privilege to help restore the predilection that the king used to show Her Highness. I think the queen would find it advantageous to entrust her allegiance to me."

I smile affably, barely succeeding in keeping my knees from buckling. "It is a very generous offer."

"It is indeed. An offer Her Highness would be prudent to secure before it is too late," he enjoins while deliberately caressing a round golden ring on his finger. It is then that I recognize, with consternation, the king's signet ring, the one used to approve all royal edicts.

Haman chuckles, pleased at my reaction. "Your Highness," he bows with mocking obsequiousness and struts away with a gleeful spring in his step.

Now Haman is going to scrutinize my movements even more carefully. Somehow, though, he has not made the connection and he does not suspect me of being a Jewess. Still, I have to be doubly cautious, lest my identity be betrayed.

I heave a sigh. *How much longer will I be able to survive in the palace with my secret intact?*

CHAPTER EIGHT

And if I perish, I perish

(Esther 4:16)

I survey my chamber. From the high square windows and the colorful glazed tiles, to the white and blue drapes hanging throughout.

I mentally review the list.

The bedding checked and cleaned. Under the carpet, likewise, bread-free. The closets, cleared. The couches, the pillows, clean. All the vessels which were used with leavened food sealed in a closet, done. Radushnamuya and Maimuna should be back now from the market with all the necessary ingredients, and Hathach will provide me with Matza. Am I missing anything?

Radushnamuya and Maimuna finally come in and I brighten at their sight. "Peace unto you, were you able to procure…" The words die on my lips when I notice their ashen faces, "What happened?" I inquire, my heart pounding with alarm.

"Your Highness…" They falter.

"What is the matter?"

"Mor…Mordechai…"

My heart drops. "What about Mordechai?"

"Forgive us, Your Highness, but we saw Mordechai outside the King's Gate. We barely recognized him."

"Whatever do you mean?"

"His hair is disheveled, he is wearing sackcloth, and he's screaming like a lunatic." They lower their eyes, hesitant to convey the rest. "Forgive us, Your Highness, for saying this, but it looks like he may have lost his reason…"

An iron vise tightens around my chest, making it hard to breathe.

No, it cannot be!

"No," I croak, clutching my chest, gasping for air. "It cannot be. We have to find out what is happening. Radushnamuya," I charge. "Fetch some decent garments and bring them to Mordechai. I need him to enter the palace and tell me what is happening and why."

"Your Highness," Shulamit ventures, her brown eyes filled with apprehension. "Wouldn't that be rash? Haman may…"

"I have to risk it, I have to know. What possible tragedy could have befallen him for Mordechai to act this way?"

From what I have heard, the only time the clear-headed Mordechai I knew had acted this dramatically was when the Holy Temple was destroyed. I remember the sleepless nights Mordechai suffered, mourning the horrors he had witnessed, yet he was mindful to conceal the tormenting memories from me. It is no wonder, therefore, that my gut is clenching and writhing, leaving me as I am, anxious and afraid to even guess what might be.

"Samanbar, Maimuna, let us go to the *Bisan*. I shall await Mordechai in my usual place."

I stand under the cool shade of the cedar trees, twisting and coiling my purple silken belt around my clammy fingers, unable to contain my agitation and uneasiness.

"Radushnamuya!" I exclaim, blood draining from my face when I see her return alone with the garments in her hands. "What is the meaning of this?"

"Forgive me, Your Highness," she replies, tears welling in her big round eyes. "Mordechai refuses to accept the garments you have sent."

I grip my sash in an effort to subdue my convulsions, squeezing it tight until my knuckles whiten. Green circles and blue dots start dancing in my eyes. My maids stare at me in concern, their brows furrowed. My legs are about to give way.

"Samanbar," I breathe, motioning for her to come close. "I need to sit."

Shulamit and Radushnamuya seize my arms as I am about to collapse.

"Maimuna!"Shulamit cries out. "Quickly, fetch a couch or a stool, something!"

"Your Highness," she says, turning to me. "Shall we return to Her Majesty's chamber?"

"No, go call Hathach. I need to speak to him."

Shulamit and Radushnamuya exchange a quick nod of the head. Radushnamuya gently releases me and runs off. Her shimmering lean figure shrinks in the distance, and Shulamit is left alone to support me. Maimuna returns with two chamberlains. They are carrying a golden couch, grunting under its weight. Pearls of sweat trickle off their shaven heads. Shulamit gently sets me down. I sit limply, depleted of energy. I close my eyes and take a deep breath, willing myself to clear the haze from my mind.

"Your Highness has sent for me?" Daniel's mellifluous cadence warms me every time I hear it.

"Thank you for coming," I choke up. "Venerable sage, I need you to find out from Mordechai exactly what is happening and why," I plead. "However," I caution. "No one is to find out I have sent you."

"I will take the Western Gate, stroll through the city square, and pretend to encounter Mordechai by chance. It might take me long to report back to Your Highness."

"Whatever you deem necessary for our safety, but please, do hurry."

If time ever stopped, this would be what it feels like. I sit on the couch, surrounded by green, dotted by splashes of color, watching the shadows cast by the trees move and shrink as the sun climbs its way up the sky in a slow, painstakingly so, fashion.

"Your Highness, Hathach is coming!" Shulamit exclaims, pointing at the aged, noble figure advancing toward us.

I scrutinize Daniel's demeanor, trying to gleam some indication of hope. His somber countenance, his heavy step, and the sickly pallor of his face portend very little of it. He produces a rolled papyrus from within the folds of his tunic. It bears the royal signature, like all missives sent throughout the Empire. I open it with trembling hands.

Endless peace be unto you!

Let it be known that there is one man in our midst who is not of our place, but is of royal ancestry, of the seed of Amalek. He is among the greatest of the generation, and his name is Haman. And he has made a request of us:

"There is a people scattered and dispersed among us who are the lowliest of all peoples, but they are arrogant; they seek our harm, and their mouths are filled with curses against the king. And they refuse to acknowledge gratitude towards those who bestowed good upon them. When they went down to Egypt, Pharaoh welcomed them cordially and settled them in the best part of the land. He fed them in the years of famine and gave them the best food in his land. He had a palace to build, and they did the building. Nevertheless, he could not prevail against them. The Jews loaded mules without number with

*the Egyptians' belongings, till they emptied all Egypt
and fled. When Pharaoh heard that they had fled,
he went after them to regain his money. What did
they do to him? There was a man in their midst by
the name of Moshe, the son of Amram. With the
use of Magic, he smote the sea with a rod till the sea
became dry. Whereupon they crossed the sea. When
Pharaoh saw it, he entered after them. They pushed
him into the sea, and he and his entire army were
drowned. They did not remember the good he
bestowed upon them. Do you hear what ingrates they
were?*

Hot blood rises to my cheeks. What a
brazen and slanderous tongue Haman has!

*Further, see what they did to Amalek, my
ancestor, when he came to wage war against them.
He saw what this people did to the Egyptians who
were so kind to them. Consequently, how much more
were they to do unto the other nations.*

*Moshe, their leader, had a disciple by the name
Yehoshua, son of Nun, who was exceedingly brutal,
and utterly merciless. Said Moshe to him, 'Choose*

144

for us men and go out to wage war against Amalek.'
And they came upon the nation of Amalek, and
smote them with their incantation.

Their first king, Shaul by name, waged war
against Amalek. He killed one hundred thousand
riders among them in one day. He had no mercy on
man, woman, or child. What else did they do to
Agag, my grandfather? First, they were merciful
towards him. Then a certain man by the name
Shmuel came, severed his body, and gave his flesh as
food to the birds of the sky.

We need not fear their G-d for they have
rebelled against Him. Further, He has aged, and
Nebuchadnezzar came and burned their holy temple.
He exiled them from their soil and brought them
among us. But they have not yet changed their
repulsive practices. And although they are exiles in
our midst, they scoff at us and at the faith of our
gods.

If even the lowliest among them are offered a
cup of wine from the king, they discard the wine and
refuse to drink it, but if a fly falls in their own cup

of wine, they drink it without any qualms about it.
Do you see how arrogant they are?

And now we have come to a common resolve.
We have cast lots, to destroy them from the world,
and to determine the most suitable time for us to do
so. The puru fell on the month of Addaru, on the
thirteenth of the month, and now, when these letters
reach you, you are all to be prepared on that day to
annihilate all the Jews in our midst, young and old,
infants and women, in one day. And you are not to
leave any survivors, and their possessions are yours
for the taking."

I drop the letter as if it were a hot burning coal.
"What is this?" I stammer, indignation and fear
coursing through my body.

"They were sent today throughout all the
hundred and twenty seven provinces," Daniel informs
me. "But only for the satraps. A different missive was
sent for the populace with a general warning to be
prepared for war on the thirteenth of Addaru, though
I have my suspicions that word will leak out about the
nature of the 'enemy'. Mordechai was able to procure

himself a copy of the letter. He says, and I agree, that here in Shushan, the state of affairs may be in control, but in farther provinces, the populace may not wait until the appropriate time to strike at our brethren. He asks that you go to the king and plead on behalf of your people."

"Addaru is not for another eleven months," I contest. "Surely, in the interim, we can—"

"There is more." He holds my pleading look with a firm, unyielding gaze. "Haman offered to pay to the king's treasuries for the right to destroy the Jews, but Achashverosh has turned it down. He is only too happy to have Haman take the responsibility of ridding the Kingdom of the Jews."

So bribery is not going to work.

Achashverosh found the perfect solution to his problem. Someone to execute the task he is too cowardly to carry out.

"Do not make the mistake of thinking that this is merely a result of political machinations," Daniel exhorts me, stroking his snowy beard. "Mordechai had a vision of Haman's exchange with Achashverosh in which simultaneously Satan petitioned the King of all Kings to destroy the Jewish people, for they have abandoned him. This is not happening because Mordechai refused to bow to Haman, but because the Jews bowed to idols in the times of Nebuchadnezzar and enjoyed themselves at Achashverosh's feast. It is a decree from Heaven. Certainly, you were placed at the palace as queen for this. You must go to the K—"

"It has been thirty days now since I have been summoned to the king," I insist. "Either he is going to call on me soon, or he has been turned against me and does not wish to see me," I explain. "Either way, it is foolish and risky to go unannounced. Everyone knows no one may enter the king's private chambers uninvited, or death is assured."

"Unless the king extends his golden scepter; then your life would be spared."

"How likely would that be, if the king is cross with me?"

"Even so, we must utilize any chance to save our people, no matter how slight."

"I never said I would not do everything in my power to help," I respond with feeling. "But are there not wiser, more effective ways? We can request an audience, we can appraise the political climate and plan accordingly; the decree is not set for another year…"

"Precious Jewish lives may be at stake at this very moment. We cannot afford to wait—"

"Do you realize what going to the king of my own volition means?" I interrupt him, tears welling in my eyes.

He lowers his head, silent.

"Did you forget I am a married woman, and who my husband is?" I persist, tears flowing down my face and nose. "Until now, every time the king summoned me, I had to go, I had no choice, but if I were to go to the king of my own volition, I would be committing adultery, and according to Torah, I would never be allowed to return to my husband."

I strike at my chest, weeping. The pain I kept securely locked, deep inside, churning and burning.

"Do you know how I have endured all those years?" I cry in between sobs. "The thought that one day I would be reunited with my Pethachia; if not in this world, in the next. But if I go to the king now, I stand to lose everything…"

"Don't you think Mordechai thought about that?" Daniel susurrates, his voice imbued with tender compassion. "If anyone would have weighed the issue seriously, taking you into consideration, that would be Mordechai. How difficult it must have been for *him* to ask this of you? I know this is hard to hear and accept, but I beg you, if Mordechai is asking *you* to do this, then it must be for your own benefit, Hadassa."

I flinch at the mention of my real name. A name and a life that I have buried so deep, cast in the darkness for so long; and now, the thick walls I carefully built come tumbling down, pent up emotions rumble, rearing up to a raging tempest. I desperately want to believe that if Mordechai knew the king has not summoned me for so long, it would change his mind; or maybe he made the decision under shock, but I know in my heart, Daniel is right.

Mordechai does not think on a whim, nor would he ask me to do something that was not in my best interest.

But still...wouldn't I be doomed to fail? There must be another way!

"I still want you to return to Mordechai and convey to him what I have told you about my current situation with the king," I entreat him, a tidal wave of conflicting emotions tossing me about like a leaf in thrall to a storm.

"I really do not think it is a good idea, I may have noticed some servant spying." Daniel shakes his head vigorously. "I may be mistaken, but especially now, we cannot afford to allow Haman to discover your connection to Mordechai."

"Please, honorable sage, I am begging you, do it for me. I do not believe I am the right choice to ensure the success of the mission. If there is even a small chance he might reconsider... I need to be sure."

He sighs, shrugging his shoulders and shaking his head. "As you wish," he concedes, unconvinced.

"Thank you," I whisper.

I watch him make his way toward the Western Gate, his blue tunic glimmering in the sun. I wring my hands, a sick feeling rising from the pit of my stomach. He disappears from sight, leaving behind the colorful scenery of the *Bisan* in full spring. But I am not soothed. Suddenly, I start running in the direction that Daniel took.

Shulamit and Maimuna follow closely behind, startled. "Your Highness, perhaps we should slow to a decorous pace…"

"I need to speak to Hathach," is my curt response. How can I slow down when I have this horrific premonition gnawing at my heart?

I stop abruptly at the Western Gate, breathless, heart pounding.

Something is not right.

My eyes shift from the sphinxes' unbecoming rear, to the stone walls, to the iron gate, and then it hits me.

The guards, where are the guards?

I sprint forward, my temples searing from the hammering of my heart.

Then I see it. A clump of ragged blue linen and limbs, unnaturally contorted, lies on the ground surrounded by a small crowd of indifferent guards and onlookers.

Daniel…NO!

A blood-curdling scream rings in my ears, only my throat has frozen, and it does not feel like it came from me.

I find myself kneeling beside him. "Hathach, Hathach?" I whimper. "Please, oh, please answer me, Hathach."

A thick black stream of blood trickles out of his mouth, his face bluish gray.

"He is gone, Your Ladyship; probably died on impact," comments a guard.

"What happened?" I manage to whisper.

"Trampled by a horse, Your Ladyship."

"Who?" I breathe.

The guards shift nervously, exchanging glances.

"Who dared?" I raise my voice, shaking angrily.

The guards stammer incomprehensibly. "Forgive us, Your Highness, we were not able to tell, it happened so fast, and the old man must have lost his mind, he just ran in the horse's way. It was very unexpected." They kneel on the ground, whimpering, faces touching the ground.

Bold-faced lies, Daniel would never do that, besides his body is close to the Gate wall. There are no blood or tracking marks from the main road. Who are they covering for? What are they afraid of?

This must be Haman's doing. He is the only one whose hate would drive him to murder even a respected personage like Daniel, and whose arrogance makes him believe he can do so with impunity.

Hot tears stream down my face.

Forgive me, Daniel, you did not even want to go, but I made you. Forgive this selfish woman. My staccato sobs give way to a soft anguished wailing.

"Your Highness," Shulamit prods me gently. "We should return inside."

"No, I won't leave until Hathach is provided for. Go fetch Nechemia. No one should touch him, we don't know what laws the Jews have pertaining death, and Hathach deserves our greatest respect, even in death," I order to no one in particular.

"Your highness, I will stay with Hathach, but Her Majesty must return to her chambers," she urges, throwing concerned glances about her.

I know Shulamit is right; if I insist in staying, the rumors may grow out of control and it will certainly jeopardize my situation. In spite of myself, I do as Shulamit has suggested, not before instructing her to make sure the message Hathach had to convey would still reach its destination.

I return to my private chamber, thoroughly spent. Images of Daniel's death mask flash before me, chilling me to the core.

I let Maimuna and Radushnamuya undress me, my clothes smudged with dirt and blood. They gently clean my hands, while I stare, glassy-eyed, into nowhere.

I have blood on my hands, Daniel's blood.

Tears spring anew.

Will you ever forgive me, Father in Heaven?

Shulamit enters my chamber, breathless.

I breathe a sigh of relief. *Thank HaShem, she is safe.*

She kneels before me and kisses my hand. "Your Highness, Hathach's burial will take place in a relatively short while. I have arranged for your attendance."

"Thank you."

"Your message was received, and I have been entrusted with a reply. I have memorized it word for word."

I stand up to receive the message, trembling. "You may begin."

Shulamit clears her throat and, eyes closed, starts reciting Mordechai's message, mimicking his mannerism, cadence, and inflections. A deep crease forms between her eyebrows as she concentrates.

"Tell the queen as follows: As soon as I became aware of the decree, I stopped children coming out of *Cheder*, and inquired as to what they had learned today. I wanted to discern whether there was still hope for the Jewish nation as a people of HaShem. One child quoted Proverbs, saying 'Do not fear sudden terror nor the destruction of the wicked when it comes.' A second child quoted Isaiah: 'Contrive a scheme but it will be foiled, conspire a plot but it will not materialize for HaShem is with us.' A third child said: 'To your old age I am with you, unto your hoary years I will sustain you. I have made you and I will carry you; I will sustain you and deliver you.' They are all prophetic answers to Haman's threat. We only need to repent and return to HaShem, and salvation will come; but you, Esther, what will become of you? If you remain silent at this time, you and the House of your Father will be lost. Perhaps it was precisely for this moment that HaShem has made you queen of Persia and Media."

If you remain silent at this time, you and the House of your Father will be lost. What does Mordechai mean by that?

"Say it again."

I have her repeat it three times until I have it seared into my memory. Yet some of his message's meaning still eludes me. Mordechai feels that I am precisely the one to fulfill this task, and if I were to refuse, I and my ancestors would be lost? I reflect on those words, tossing them around from every angle, endeavoring to uncover their implications.

"Your Highness?" Shulamit's arms are outstretched, a scroll in her open palms, she raises them toward me like an offering. "Mordechai thought that within these words, you will find the resolve you seek."

I roll it open. It is Jeremaiah's prophesies.

So says the Lord: I remember the loving kindness of your youth, the love of your nuptials, your following me in the desert, in a land not sown... What wrong did your forefathers find in Me, that they distanced themselves from Me, and they went after futility?...Truly, as a woman betrays her beloved, so have you betrayed Me, O house of Israel...

Indeed, when we accepted the Torah at Mount Sinai, we were bound with HaShem like a woman to her husband. We swore our undying devotion and faithfulness, yet we have betrayed Him by placing our trust in idols or humans. The truth is that our betrayal is only skin deep. Yes, Jews have bowed to idols, but not sincerely; they have sought to ingratiate themselves and seek protection and security from a human king, and affronted HaShem's honor by doing so. Even so, I believe that deep inside every Jewish heart beats that same unwavering loyalty of a star-struck newlywed. It only needs to be revealed.

And you will seek Me with all your heart, and I will be found by you, says HaShem.

Is this why Mordechai asks me to endanger my life? For only an extraordinary act of sacrifice will bring to the fore the unbreakable love bond we share with HaShem?

I pause; the intensity of that thought overwhelms me. Then, as if calling to me, the words draw me in again.

The prophet who has a dream, let him tell a dream, and who has My word, let him tell My word as truth.

Like a flash of light in the darkness, I have an epiphany. All is crystal clear: my dream, its meaning, and Mordechai's words.

When my ancestor, King Shaul, was commanded by HaShem, through the prophet Shmuel, to eradicate Amalek, he was told to leave no remembrance. Yet King Shaul was swayed by his own reason and emotions, and failed to carry out his divine mandate. He spared Agag, the king, and some animals.

In my vivid dream, Agag turns into a deadly snake and strikes at King Shaul mercilessly. And now, a descendant of Amalek is poised to strike all Jews.

I break out in a cold sweat and a shiver runs down my spine as I relive King Shaul's eyes staring from his bloody face, calling out to me, pleading to help him.

Is this then what the dream means? I must correct my great grandfather's mistake? And it must be me, for if I refuse, *I and my ancestors will be lost.* I will have forfeited the opportunity to rectify King Shaul's fault.

The musty scroll beckons me once more.

A voice is heard on high, lamentation, bitter weeping, Rachel weeping for her children, she refuses to be comforted for her children for they are not. So says the Lord: Refrain your voice from weeping and your eyes from tears, for there is reward for your work, and they shall come back from the land of the enemy.

I recall the days when Pethachia and I, poring over the scriptures, would recount the lore of what lies in between the terse verses. How I loved to hear the deeds of our Matriarchs, and how I wished to emulate them.

The Patriarchs and the Matriarchs went to appease the Holy One, blessed be He, concerning the sin of Manasseh who placed an image in the Temple but He was not appeased. Rachel entered and stated before Him, "O Lord of the Universe, whose mercy is greater, Your mercy or the mercy of a flesh and blood person? You must admit that Your mercy is greater. Now did I not bring my rival into my house? For all the work that Jacob worked for my father, he worked only for me. When I came to enter the nuptial canopy, they brought my sister, and it was not enough that I kept my silence, but I gave her my password. You, too, if Your children have brought Your rival into Your house, keep Your silence for them." He said to her, "You have defended them well. There is reward for your deed and for your righteousness, that you gave over your password to your sister."

Was that the reason Rachel was buried on the road to Ephrath, alone, so that she could intervene on behalf of her children when they were being exiled? Did she know she was the only one who could? Did she foresee in the throes of labor that her children would need her, and that is why, as she was dying, she named her child "Ben Oni", son of my sorrow?

The magnitude of her sacrifice moves me to tears and I am overtaken by a burst of gasping spasms.

I know without a doubt what I must do, but I will not act alone. I find Haman's letter and reread it with care. The answer to our predicament is to be found in his accusations. He says "a people scattered and dispersed", then the solution must be to come together in unison. He says "arrogant", then we need to humble ourselves through fast and prayer. Haman cast a puru, lotteries, surrendering his scheme to a plane of inescapable fate, beyond calculations or logic. We, too, must employ effort beyond reason and prove to HaShem that our commitment and relationship with Him reaches far beyond sense. No matter what the cost, we shall not give up our Jewish identity. That is why I will go to the king, uninvited, and reveal I am a Jewess, and plead for my people.

"Your Highness, your entourage is ready to accompany you to the funeral," Shulamit informs me, her voice a respectful whisper, almost afraid to interrupt my inner contemplation.

I sigh, nod, and exit my chamber. A closed carriage awaits me, though Daniel's burial will not be distant. Just outside the palace walls, in the royal city, a mausoleum will be built, as befits a man who served the kings of his time with exemplary integrity.

"HER MAJESTY, THE QUEEN!" The crier announces my arrival. A throng of wailing mourners is already in attendance. Mordechai is at their head, wearing sackcloth and gray ashes on his head.

His voice hoarse and broken, he urges the people to return to the righteous path, to reconnect to HaShem, for the death of a *Tzadik*, a saintly person, atones just like Yom Kippur.

With a loud cry, he proclaims, "Blessed are You, King of the Universe, *Dayan Emeth*, the True Judge."

Following his lead, the crowd erupts in deafening howls of sobbing and wailing.

My heart is throbbing and my eyes are stinging, but I must maintain my composure.

I instruct Shulamit to pass on to a trusted person a message to be relayed to Mordechai. To gather all the Jewish people in fast and prayer for three days, that they may pray for me for the sin of having caused Daniel's death, and the sins I will be committing by going willingly to the king.

I watch Mordechai's reaction as he receives my message; a dark line furrows his forehead, something perplexes him about my request.

He approaches me. "Forgive us, Your Highness, for our attire and distress. Great is your graciousness for having come to pay respect to our late Hathach," he says, bowing his head. "Three days?" he mutters under his breath. "In three days, it will be *Pesach*, shall we fast on the *Seder* night?" he asks incredulously.

"Sage of Israel!" I reply respectfully, but exasperated. "What is there to celebrate on *Pesach* if there will be no more Jews?"

Better fast this Pesach and ensure our survival so that we may yet celebrate many more Passovers to come.

Mordechai nods his agreement, still keeping his head bowed. "I will do as you ask; I have already gathered twenty-two thousand children—"

"Actually, when I asked to gather all Jews, I meant all. Sinners and assimilated Jews as well."

He is motionless for a moment, trying to process my directive. "Can we expect irreligious Jews to fast for three days; can they really change so suddenly? Besides, it is precisely their errant behavior that has aroused HaShem's wrath; how can they bring salvation? That which incriminates cannot act as defense."

"On the contrary, it is precisely the sinners that will annul the decree by uncovering their true essence, by showing HaShem our hearts always stayed true to Him despite the temptations and indiscretions."

Mordechai forgets himself and meets my unwavering gaze, a mixture of awe and pride shining in his eyes.

"Tzadka mimeni." She is more righteous than I, he says. My heart misses a beat; my defenses are dangerously close to coming undone.

"My maids and I shall fast as well, and in three days, I shall go to the king," I murmur. *And if that means I stand to lose you, I will lose you.*

"You are dismissed, you may go," I say, confused, my voice shriller than I intended.

"May the Creator bless you, Your Highness," he says, bowing with deference.

I respond with a cold, nigh imperceptible nod, and rush to take cover in my insulated carriage, lest I lose all dignity in front of everyone.

Within the safe, upholstered walls of the *harmamaxae*, I allow some silent tears, but I will myself to reserve the storm brewing inside for the confines of my private chamber.

"Samanbar," I call. "I need you to carry out an important mission for me."

"Your wish is my command, Your Majesty."

"Please take all the necessary precautions, for it will entail some danger."

She grasps my hand and kisses it. "It shall be done, my queen," she declares with steely determination in her eyes.

I watch her departure, a fervent prayer on my lips, a heavy stone weighing on my heart.

CHAPTER NINE

And the king extended to Esther the golden scepter that was in his hand

(Esther 5:2)

I fall upon my face and cry. I plead, I beg, and I cry until I do not have any tears left to cry. And then I cry some more.

G-d of Israel, Creator of the world, Who has dominion for eternity! Help your lowly maidservant, for I am an orphan, without father and mother.

Ever since I can remember, HaShem has been my rock, my refuge. He was my father and my mother, for I had never known them. Whenever I felt

169

scared, lonely, or overwhelmed, HaShem was the one I turned to. Hadn't Mordechai taught me that HaShem always answers an orphan's cry?

Out of the depths, I call to You, HaShem, hearken to my pleas. If You were to preserve iniquities, My G-d, who could survive? But forgiveness is with You, that You may be held in awe.

The wiry threads of gold and the precious stones woven into the carpet prick my dry skin. Dust clings to my face, wet from tears and perspiration. My hair is ruffled and covered in ashes. Everything around me is hazed; I assume the maidservants are praying, too.

A wave of brutal images fills my mind, images of Daniel's mangled body, of his lifeless face, and my body contorts in fits of violent sobs.

Save Your flock from these enemies who have risen up against us. Father of orphans! I beseech You to stand by the right hand of this orphan, who has placed her trust in Your Loving Kindness. Grant me mercy before this man, for I fear him.

Cast him down before me, for You cast down the haughty.

"Your Majesty, please!" Shifra urges. "You must rest; you must take care of yourself!" she prods me gently to get up from the floor, but I refuse.

"No, Shifra," I say, shaking my head. "This is not about me."

Indeed, it never was and never shall be. I pass my tongue over my dry lips, my mouth parched like a desert, but she must understand. "This is about the Jewish people, and their bond with HaShem."

My heart is broken but somewhere beneath my distress, I cling to the belief and the promise that HaShem shall never forsake His people.

Israel, put your hope in HaShem, for with Him, there is kindness; with Him, there is abounding deliverance. And He will redeem Israel from all its iniquities.

The morning of the third day, I rise from the floor and gaze out the window. The sky is clear and a bright orange sun is climbing up behind the mountains; birds are chirping and chasing each other through the trees.

Today is the day.

I breathe in deeply and let the morning breeze fill my lungs.

Though I walk in the valley of the shadow of death, I will fear no evil, for You are with me.

A certain sense of peace and purpose has descended into my heart and replaced the utter desperation I have felt these past few days.

I turn to my attendants; they, too, have kept their pledge of fast and prayer, I see it in their gaunt faces. Though their eyes are surrounded by dark circles, they shine feverishly as they look to me for guidance.

"Where is Samanbar?" I ask.

"I'm here, Your Majesty, faithfully by your side," she answers, bowing.

"Has HaShem granted you success in the mission I entrusted you with?" I whisper softly.

"He has, my queen."

"Bless you. Let us not waste any time then."

She leads me to a chest, and my heart trembles in anticipation to uncover its content. Part of me wonders why I insisted on it when it entailed needless risks, but there is a deeper part of me that feels unprepared to face what lays ahead without it. She must have procured it with much pain and subterfuge, and I am grateful to her for it.

It takes three of us to open the chest, for our fasts have weakened us considerably.

There it is.

The most exquisite robe, the likes of which had never been seen before in all of Persia and Media. It is of soft linen, the color of a spring morning sky with a sash of purple velvet hemmed with delicate golden pomegranates. Clasped at the shoulders by small rubies, the sash wraps the chest with elegance and then falls delicately on the sides.

I let my fingers run through the velvety sash with reverence; this dress was worn by royalty, my ancestress in the House of King Shaul.

"I will wear it today, when I go to the king."

For today, I will go to the king of my own volition and reveal to him who I am. Today, I shall restore the name of the house of my father. Today, I shall approach HaShem, the King of all Kings, and sacrifice everything I am.

The maidservants proceed to bathe and prepare me. They rub my skin with fragrant oil, massaging me with leaves and petals. Their mood is somber, but my heart is strong. I'm determined and unwavering; I shall surrender my body and my soul for the sake of my people.

With the crown on my head, in full royal panoply and flanked by my trusted maidservants, I approach the royal chamber. I am ready, HaShem is with me.

There are seven doors that precede the Throne Room, and though the guards stare at us, unsure, they let us through unchallenged. Yet, as we reach the inner court facing the Throne Room, my steps become heavier and my breathing shallow.

Facing me, brooding morosely, the king sits, wearing royal crimson robes, the purple tiara, and holding the golden scepter. He is surrounded by his ministers, officers, and the imposing idols that adorn the court.

I feel faint, my strength deserts me, and suddenly, my legs cannot hold me.

My G-d, my G-d, why have You forsaken me!

I can see the guards closing in, unsheathing their swords, waiting for a nod from the king, greed shining in their eyes as they lust after my precious stones and clothing.

HaShem, do not be distant; my Strength, hurry to my aid! Save me!

I meet the king's eyes and they are incandescent with fury. I have defied him and dared to appear uninvited. Shulamit, supporting me on the right, starts weeping silently.

I fall on my knees, shaking, awaiting the blow of the sword or the brutal grasp of the guards. I should be confessing before meeting my Maker, but I cannot form a single coherent thought.

"His Majesty is asking you a question. Respond at once!" The barking order jolts me and I suddenly become aware the king is touching me, wrapping his big ungainly arms around my neck and shoulders.

"Esther, queen of my heart! Why have you placed yourself in such jeopardy, to come here now?" he asks in a subdued growl, moved and concerned. "Do not be afraid. You are my queen, nothing will happen to you!" He extends his golden scepter and my trembling hands grope for it; but I cannot say a word, my voice has frozen inside my throat and I cannot let a sound out.

"What is it, my beloved queen, why do you look so pale? What is troubling you that you should risk your life? Tell me, my dear, what is your request, and I shall grant it. Even if it is half my Kingdom, it shall be given to you!" There is apprehension in his voice, but I still have not regained my composure, as I'm trembling uncontrollably.

Shetar, the interpreter, nears hesitantly. Unsure whether he should interfere or not; the king's moods fluctuate so violently, it makes it hard to guess what action will please him and what will send one to a premature death.

"If...if it pleases...the king," My tongue is numb, but I will myself to form the words with coherence. "Let the king...and Haman come today to a banquet I have prepared for him."

The king doesn't answer immediately; Shetar takes the silence as a cue to translate. "The queen wishes to invite His Majesty the king and Haman to a feast prepared in His Majesty's honor."

I can detect a hint of disappointment and surprise in the king's silence; nevertheless, he magnanimously extends his scepter again and places it on my head as a gesture of benevolence.

"So shall it be done, as my queen wishes. Let Haman not tarry!" he thunders.

"The king accepts the queen's invitation," Shetar announces.

I bow, my legs still trembling, and turn to leave.

It is only when we reach the safety of my chamber that I allow myself to feel the full impact of what had just transpired. I drop on the couch, shivering.

"What now, Your Majesty?" Shifra asks, reminding me that I cannot afford to be affected by my emotions.

I sigh. "If we wish to have success, we must explore all the possibilities, one may never know from whence salvation will come. We must not make the mistake of underestimating our enemy; Haman is sly, slippery. Better to keep him close than give him a chance to slip away. Was he not the one who brought the demise of the king's beloved Vashti, and was he not sentenced to death for it? Not only did he manage to escape unscathed, but he eventually secured for himself the highest position in the realm. Even if I were to convince Achashverosh to eliminate Haman, the king is too fickle and Haman is too cunning. We cannot trust that the king will follow through. Better to play on Achashverosh's insecurities, let him become jealous of the attention Haman is receiving from me, the queen, and then w—"

"But then the king might kill you both!" exclaims Radushnamuya in horror, interrupting me.

"Death would be oh, so sweet to me, compared to this life I'm living, trapped in this golden prison," I reply with fervor. "We need to mar the trust Haman enjoys and turn the king against him."

I suspect that as careful as we had been, Haman may have guessed my ties to Mordechai. Better keep him happy and off guard, lest he kills the king and usurp the throne; he has tried it before, and that's uppermost in his mind. Moreover, all this honor bestowed on Haman is going to make him even more conceited and he won't resist the temptation to preen at court, which, in turn, is going to augment the jealousy and resentment many ministers and officers already feel towards him.

I heave a deep sigh. What an empty life the palace offers. I've lived here for five years and there seems to be no rest for the aristocracy within it; they conspire against each other to gain some fleeting power. But it can be expedient and I must use it to my advantage.

And to think that there are Jews who thought they could count on the king for protection, if only they would acquiesce to his whims! Let them think that I'm trying to save only my life by ingratiating myself to the enemy. Let them realize that HaShem is their only answer, the one they should turn to for salvation.

*   *   *

"HIS ROYAL HIGHNESS, HIS MAJESTY, THE KING!" the crier announces.

My heart beats with trepidation as the royal entourage enters my chamber.

"Please be seated, my honored guests." I bow my head, showing the way to the gold-inlaid couches. The table is bursting with precious tableware filled with aromatic delicacies. I pour wine into the king's and Haman's rhytons.

"If I may be so bold, Your Majesty, allow your humble servant to toast to the queen's beauty and charm," Haman gushes, his voice dripping with sticky sap.

I feel the need to wash with cold water.

The king grunts his agreement before downing his wine in a few gulps.

They both seem to be enjoying themselves; they fail to realize I have not touched any of the food or drink, for I intend to keep my fast until the end of the day.

A soft, sweet melody fills the chamber as Aryaina's nimble fingers dance along the harp.

"To my lovely queen!" Achashverosh cheers, extending his goblet for another refill.

He seems eager to please me. I am well aware that his not knowing what I have in mind perturbs him; he cannot begin to guess what I want and that scares him, considering his need to feel in control. Perhaps he fears that I might ask him the one thing he has vowed never to do, that is, allowing the Temple to be rebuilt.

Haman, on the other hand, is not plagued by any concern. He is in very high spirits and sometimes, his attitude borders on the insolent. When I catch his gaze, I lower my eyes with a hint of a smile on my lips; the arrogant buffoon that he is, he is going to think that I desire him.

"Esther, my beloved queen, now that we are here, tell me what is your wish and I shall grant it."

My heart pounds and my hands become clammy. I look at Haman lying pompously on the couch, merrily feasting with the king, and I know instinctively that the time is not right.

"What I want...What I wish...," I stammer, afraid all our efforts and dreams might be dashed in one blow. "Let the king and Haman come to another banquet I shall prepare for them tomorrow," I say hastily. I just cannot bring myself to ask the king; I need a sign from heaven that our prayers have been answered.

Shetar is about to start "translating" when the king raises his hand, annoyed at his interference, but then, glancing at Haman and back at Shetar, he motions at the latter to continue, albeit halfheartedly.

"The queen requests the king and Haman's presence again tomorrow for another feast she has prepared for them." Shetar is sweating profusely, and he wipes his forehead and pronounced chin with a linen cloth, plucked hastily from his belt.

"Surely that is not why you risked your life, to invite me to a party," Achashverosh rumbles, annoyed, but he can see I'm flustered. He reaches for my hand and says kindly, "Do not be afraid, Esther. I shall grant you half of my kingdom if that is what you wish."

I hold his gaze. "If I have found favor in the king's eyes, and if the king wishes to fulfill my request, let the king and Haman come again tomorrow. Then I shall reveal what the king desires to know."

The royal retinue finally leaves. I let myself fall on the couch to collect my thoughts. There is still much that needs to be done before I retire for the night and I am exhausted.

"Radushnamuya, please instruct the cooks as to the food that needs to be prepared for tomorrow's feast." I take a deep breath. Suddenly, I have an urge to hold my son tightly in my arms. "Samanbar, Shifra, I wish to go by the King's Gate; I believe Prince Darius should be there."

"Should we summon the Crown Prince to come to your chambers? You have been through a lot today."

"No, I would rather walk there; the evening air will do me good."

The crickets are chirping, the trees are swaying in the gentle breeze. The round moon is visible in the sky, though it is barely dusk.

"Shhh, do you hear that?" I whisper; there is a faint noise that contrasts the peaceful mood of the evening.

Shulamit and Shifra shake their heads.

I strain to extricate the sound and identify it. *Is it wailing or the bleating of sheep?*

Before Shulamit and Shifra can protest, I start quickly in the direction of the sound.

I am wholly unprepared for the sight that meets my eyes. Right at the King's gate, hundreds of small children, Jewish children, are being led in chains. Guards are trying to stop the flow of mothers who are struggling to reach their sons. The guards beat them, but some undeterred mothers make it to their chained children. They hold bread in their hands and plead with the children to at least eat before they are brought to their death on the morrow. But these sweet young ones, with fiery devotion in their eyes, refuse. They have pledged to Mordechai they would fast for three days, and so they would fast till the end.

My heart aches, and hot tears stream down my face.

Father in Heaven, shall you remain silent even now?

I wipe my tears, pat my cheeks, and, affecting my most authoritative stance, I approach the guards. "Who are these children, and what are you doing with them?"

The guards bow. "They are Jewish children, Your Ladyship. They have committed a crime against the honorable Haman, and are to be executed at dawn."

A crime against Haman? And what was their crime, being Jews?

I look at the children, sweet boys with long side-locks swaying and the tassels hanging from beneath their tunics. Some are as young as my son; they cling to the older boys, maybe eight to ten year olds, big innocent eyes filled with fear but determination.

The starkness of his evil blasts me in the face. His hate is not like any other. Yes, Achashverosh hates the Jews and their G-d, but his hate is born out of conceit and cowardice, the need to be all powerful and the fear that the Almighty might demand from him what he does not wish to give.

"What possible threat can these little children pose to such a powerful person as Haman?" I challenge, indignant. "As queen of this empire, I demand a stay of execution until further evidence is brought to light."

"Forgive us, Your Highness, but this is Haman's jurisdiction, we dare not disobey his orders."

"You mean the great Viceroy handled this matter in person?" I sneer.

"He did, Your Highness."

"Is there a problem, Your Highness?" inquires a soft voice behind me.

I turn to see Charvona, one of the king's advisors and a close associate of Haman. He is a squat man with bushy eyebrows and balding round head. "What is the commotion about?" he asks placidly.

"Are you aware these children are to be executed tomorrow?"

"I am, Your Ladyship. They have committed a grave offense against His Majesty."

"Against His Majesty, or Haman?"

"Yes, Your Highness, by sinning against a person whom the king holds in high esteem, they have sinned against the king."

I hold myself from scoffing, and eye Charvona. Though he works closely with Haman, he does not strike me as faction-driven, more of an opportunist.

Perhaps, if I can convince him Haman's power is ephemeral, he may be swayed to switch alliances.

"Tomorrow, I am entertaining His Majesty and Haman at a private banquet. I shall be gratified if you halt execution at least until after the feast."

Charvona hesitates.

"I will be sure to mention you to His Majesty favorably."

"I suppose it can be done," he says, scratching his double chin.

"I shall be indebted to you."

I turn away, my emotions in turmoil. *Have I missed my chance? Will these children be saved?*

I know the look on these children's eyes will haunt me tonight.

"Samanbar, Shifra, let us return to my chamber at once," I murmur in a broken voice.

"What about the Crown Prince?"

"How can I embrace my own son, when countless mothers are crying for theirs who are to be executed tomorrow?" I swallow hard. "Let us return to my chamber and storm the Heavens so that the children may be returned to their mothers in health and happiness."

CHAPTER TEN

Grant me my life as my wish, and my people as my request

(Esther 7:3)

"Your Highness! Your Highness!" Shulamit's soft whisper and gentle touch stir me from my sleep. I must have fallen into sleep after having spent the night in prayer and supplication.

I look up to see Shulamit's eyes brimming with excitement. "Your Highness, your prayer has been accepted Above!"

"What are you talking about?"

"Achashverosh has ordered Haman to reward Mordechai for having saved his life five years ago. You remember, Bigthan and Theresh? They tried poisoning the king, and Mordechai told you about it, and you told the king? Anyway, Haman is to dress Mordechai with the royal garb, mount him on the king's horse, and lead him around the capital announcing 'so shall be done to the man whom the king wishes to honor'." She claps her hands, giggling infectiously, and I find myself smiling along with her.

"Haman is to lead him around the capital? How and why?" It is hard to believe that the Viceroy, second to the king, should be relegated to such a duty. Could it be that Haman is finally beginning his ruin?

"Your scheme of getting the king jealous and suspicious of Haman must be bearing fruit. Patiaspa, the king's gardener, said the king seemed mightily annoyed that Haman had ordered the trees from the royal garden to be cut for the gallows he plans to prepare for Mordechai. And Anzuka, the king's personal servant, said the king could hardly contain his rage when Haman suggested the royal garb and horse that was used for his coronation should be used to honor a very dear subject of the king." She shakes her head, sighing. "Only Haman could get away with suggesting such a thing without being accused of treason. Anzuka thinks the king now is weary of Haman, and suspects the man might have designs on the Crown."

A mischievous smile spreads on her lips. "Poor fool," she sneers. "He must have thought the king meant himself when he said he had a dear subject he wished to honor, certainly not Mordechai!"

"But how did it suddenly occur to the king to reward Mordechai now, after five years?"

"Anzuka says the king could not fall asleep, so he ordered the Palace Chronicles to be read to him, and it came to the page where it recounted how Mordechai uncovered the plot to assassinate the king, but there was no recording of a reward having been bestowed. That disturbed the king, because he is afraid it will discourage other subjects from coming forward. Then Haman came, and the king felt he should ask his advice on—"

"Samanbar," I exclaim, now fully awake. "Quick, send a missive for the capital to close all their businesses and proclaim a national holiday. I want everyone to behold Mordechai's reward. Maimuna, please help me dress, I would like to view the procession from the best spot the palace has to offer."

It isn't too long before I am able to watch from afar, Mordechai, resplendent in royal blue garments, riding with a shining countenance. Runners in colorful tunics precede him, playing flutes and drums. I sigh with contentment, my heart fluttering.

My help comes from HaShem, Maker of heaven and earth.

This is the sign I was waiting for. HaShem will certainly deliver the enemy into my hands, and today, I shall succeed.

The banquet shall be held in the Apadna. I stride with confidence, concealing the apprehension that simmers inside, letting the tapping of my golden slippers drown out all other sounds or thoughts.

The vast hall is bedecked extravagantly for the occasion. Embroidered purple drapes, dyed with the precious dye from the sea, hang from the columns, giving our banquet area a pretense of privacy. A fragrant breeze of spring in bloom wafts in from the nearby Bisan. Achashverosh, sitting on the edge of the couch, taps his foot impatiently.

"Well, send for him, how dare he make the queen wait?" He barks at the servants. He heaves a sigh and plops a few dates in his mouth. "I must admit," he says, chewing loudly. "I am curious as to why you requested his presence. Is it connected to what you are going to tell me about yourself?"

I smile enigmatically. *You cannot imagine how.*

Haman is soon brought in by two guards. He stumbles, his feet dragging, wet, foul odor dripping from his head and clothes. Haman looks forlorn and upset.

Compliments of a jeering crowd?

"Have a seat," orders Achashverosh, twisting his nose, trying to ignore the unpleasant smell.

The guards bow their heads and retreat behind the drapes, leaving only the king, Haman, and me.

Shetar stands nearby, ready to "translate" on my behalf. Despite his generous build, it is as if he is invisible, as Achashverosh and Haman carry on without acknowledging his presence at all. He seems to prefer it that way.

"Forgive my appearance, Your Majesty. I was busy carrying out the king's bidding, and I have not had a chance to prepare myself appropriately," an uncharacteristic Haman answers dejectedly.

"Fear not, Haman, you are probably the only person in this palace who can appear before the king in this manner and not be put to death immediately," I say amiably. "If there are people who cannot appreciate the esteem and power you wield at the palace, then that is their unfortunate problem." I see my words are having their desired effect, as Haman literally transforms before my eyes. His haughty gleam returns, he puffs up his chest, probably telling himself how right I am, that he is the most powerful man in the world, and he'll let those people who dared jeer at him pay dearly.

Pleased with himself, encouraged by my flattery, he starts stuffing his mouth with fruits, cheeses, and wine, too engrossed to notice that King Achashverosh is not likewise enjoying himself, and is eying him with hostility. He holds the rhyton by the lion shape and swirls the wine pensively, almost frowning. Then he turns his attention to me, attempting to appear cheerful.

"My dear queen, what is on your mind? Whatever you wish, I shall grant it, up to half my kingdom."

I kneel in front of the king, tears streaming down my face. In my mind, I am addressing the King of all Kings, whose Power and Mercy are everlasting. "My king, if I have found favor in your eyes, if the king cares for me at all, please spare my life and the lives of my people."

"What?!" Achashverosh chokes, splattering wine all over himself. "Spare your life? What are you saying?"

"My people and I have been marked for extermination. Had we been sold to slavery, I would have kept my silence, for then the king's loss would not have been as damaging."

"What are you talking about? Who would dare to threaten you?"

I look up and stare Achashverosh in the eyes.

You.

You desired my people's demise just as he did, and you were too happy to allow it. Did you not give your ring and full liberty to Haman to carry out the deed?

I want to point at him and scream it. Instead, I point at Haman. "This evil man, *Haman!*"

I stand tall and lift my chin, "I am Hadassa, daughter of Avichail, from the House of King Shaul, of the tribe of Benjamin," I proclaim. "I am a Jewess, and together with my people, we have been sentenced to extermination by this hateful man!"

An eerie silence follows. Achashverosh is reeling with shock from my revelation, the full implications involved have not yet taken root. He is still grappling with the discovery. I hope he will appreciate the significance of it, that his own son is a Jew, and maybe not hate the Jews for fear they might snatch his throne.

Haman has risen from the couch. He is sweating profusely, and is unable to find words to extricate himself from the accusation. He keeps turning from me to the king, unsure of whom he should address.

Shetar is dumbfounded, too. His mouth is wide open, but no "translation" is forthcoming. Finally, he recovers and starts stuttering "Er...the queen is...uhm..."

"Silence, you fool!" Achashverosh roars, striking a quivering Shetar dumb. The "Interpreter" shrinks into himself, willing to disappear.

"I won't be needing your services. Did you not hear? The queen is of royal blood. I will be conversing with her directly," he bellows. Confused, intoxicated by the wine, and unable to contain his fury, Achashverosh storms out of the Apadna into the Bisan, presumably to recollect his wits.

The moment we are left alone, Haman throws himself at my feet, groveling. "Your Highness, most gracious queen, forgive this humble servant. I did not know. I never would have dared to send out such a decree. I deserve to be punished, but I beseech you, merciful queen, forgive me just this once, or at least, spare my children, my family, they do not deserve to suffer on my account." Tears flow from his eyes, and though I know they are all lies, his cries tug at my heart, and I waver.

My great grandfather's pleading eyes come to mind and the sad innocent faces of the young chained boys. I steel myself anew, and turn my face away.

In a flash, Haman's eyes transform from pleading and pitiful to angry and hateful. "You filthy Jewess, you are all the same," he hisses.

He grabs my shoulders and shakes me. "You think you have defeated me? I am Haman, son of Hamedatha, the Agagite. If I am to fall, you shall fall along with me." He throws me on the couch, and while keeping my wrists pinned, he snarls into my ear, "Do you think your dear king will spare you when he sees you cavorting with his Viceroy?"

The shock of the assault and sheer terror has rendered me incapacitated. My body is on fire. I cannot move a limb or shout, much less breathe.

"**Will you violate my queen in my own home**?!" Achashverosh's terrifying roar has Haman stumbling off the couch and stuttering incoherently.

Guards and chamberlains appear at the king's bellows. Shulamit and Maimuna run to my side. I'm lying on the couch, unable to move, gasping for air, tears stinging my eyes. My chest heaving, I explode in a torrent of gasping sobs, shaking.

Achashverosh, still fuming, eyes me with a hard, inscrutable face.

The guards, clutching a whimpering Haman, await the king's order.

Charvona comes forward. "Your Majesty, if I may, Haman has erected a fifty-cubits-high gallows, on which he planned to hang Mordechai, the very same man the king honored earlier today."

"Hang him on it!" Achashverosh barks, pointing at Haman. "*At once!*"

Immediately, the guards cover Haman's face with a black hood, and drag him away.

Achashverosh plops on the couch, his rage finally abating. He glances at me again, this time with concern in his eyes. "Take her to her quarters and send for a healer," he grunts.

"Yes, Your Majesty," my maidservants reply, curtsying.

They carry me away, Achashverosh brooding behind my stumbling progress.

Blessed is my Rock Who delivered me from the man of violence. I will sing to HaShem for He has dealt kindly with me.

CHAPTER ELEVEN

Venahafoch hu, and it was just the opposite

(Esther 9:1)

"What does Her Highness think?" Maimuna holds up a mirror, after having fixed my pearl encrusted headpiece and painted my eyes.

"Thank you, Maimuna." I oblige her with a perfunctory glance at the mirror. "Nicely done."

She frowns. "Her Majesty has lost too much weight," she sighs. "Perhaps a walk in the Bisan will calm Her Highness' heart?"

I demur. These days, the Bisan does not provide for me the escape it used to afford me, as Haman's gallows is visible from most parts of the palace. Presumably, he built it so because he wished to exult and gloat at the demise of his archenemy at any given moment. Perhaps he even planned to have the king himself hang on that gallows. Whatever the case, I derive no pleasure in seeing his carcass hanging. It evokes traumatic memories I'd rather forget. I do understand, though, why Achashverosh has ordered Haman's body to hang in display all this time. It is to serve as a warning to anyone who espouses Haman's aspirations. Yet reports prove otherwise. Enemies of the Jews are gathering weapons with every intention to carry out Haman's wishes. Though the war against Haman has been delivered into my hands, the war against the Enemies of the Jews has yet to be dealt with. The decree still looms over our head like a cobra poised to strike.

"Blessing unto you, Your Highness." The chamberlains have come to escort me to the king. They stand, heads bowed, at the entrance of my chamber, waiting.

"Let us go," I say, my heart quickening with trepidation. *Will the king acquiesce this time and overturn the decree?*

It is the law of the land that a decree signed by the king may not be rescinded. I did try to impress upon the king, however, that, in truth, the decree was mandated by Haman, who withheld important details from the king, so it could not really be said that the decree was authorized by the king. Achashverosh, though, is not convinced. I think he believes revoking the decree for that reason will make him look weak in the eyes of the people, that he allowed himself to be swindled by Haman.

Mordechai thinks it is prudent to wait and measure how we approach Achashverosh. He does not believe the king suddenly will become a Jew-lover, even though his own son is one. Achashverosh will, as he always has, do what is politically expedient for him.

I worry how we are going to overcome these hurdles, so I am relieved Mordechai is at my side. The king has appointed him as Viceroy instead of Haman.

I have only disclosed that I am a cousin to Mordechai, but Achashverosh must suspect we were more than that. Perhaps Achashverosh feels more comfortable having Mordechai close by, to monitor him.

"HER MAJESTY, THE QUEEN!" the crier announces as I am ushered into the Throne Room. The bas reliefs portraying the king fighting with lions shimmers by the light of the fire that is burning in the tall torches. Achashverosh sits on the throne, surrounded by advisors and guards, golden scepter in his right hand. He acknowledges me with a nod and hint of a smile. Mordechai, standing at his right, remains stone-faced, but his eyes dance with a gleam only I can see, fortifying me with strength and courage.

I kneel, and though the king has already acknowledged me, I remain kneeling, eyes tearing. "My king," I choke up. "You have been most gracious to me, but how can my heart be at peace, when Haman's evil plot still threatens the Jews?"

"I have already hanged Haman because he attempted to harm the Jews. I have given you his estate, and appointed Mordechai in his stead. That should be sufficient to deter the enemies."

"I wish it were so, but I have received reports that Haman's wife, Zeresh, and his sons are rallying support to create an army to carry out the decree at all costs. If I am good in the king's eyes, let an order be written to withdraw the letter written by Haman calling for the extermination of the Jews."

"I cannot retract the decree. It is the law."

You can do so if you want. You don't wish to.

"Gracious king, permit me to interject," Mordechai says. "The decree stated what the people had to do to the Jews, but it did not say what the Jews could do."

"What do you mean?"

"The general populace received note to be prepared for war on the thirteenth of Addaru, but it did not specify the enemy. Only the satraps were made aware of it. It has been now two months, and the couriers should be expected to have returned. Let us send out again the same couriers with a missive allowing the Jews to arm themselves to defend their lives. Let them clear any confusion or misunderstanding, and explain to the satraps that the king suspected Haman's loyalty and allowed those first missives to draw out the true enemy. For whoever insists in attacking the Jews, even when the king supports them, is rebelling against the Crown."

"By Mithra, that's right! Let the Jews do whatever they must to defend themselves. Not only I shall allow it, I approve of it," Achashverosh exclaims, happy he'll be able to keep his dignity intact. Indeed, Mordechai cleverly afforded the king the opportunity to explain the recent contradictions with a seamless, brilliant solution.

"Here is my ring," the king says, handing Mordechai the signet ring he had previously trusted Haman with. "You may write an amendment regarding the Jews as you see fit and seal it with my name."

"Your Majesty," Mordechai says, bowing while accepting the ring. "Your kindness knows no bounds."

*　　*　　*

From my favorite spot in the Bisan, flanked by the proud cedar trees, I can discern the deep bleating of the dromedaries of the royal stock, specially bred for running. Today, the couriers are being sent again throughout the one-hundred-and-twenty-seven provinces of the Empire with the new missives dictated by Mordechai.

Nechemia, his thin frame, stooped shoulders, and scraggly beard, stands before me.

"Your Highness," he says respectfully. "You have summoned me?"

"Yes, I wish to be apprised of every detail of the current situation," I assert. "I know Mordechai has sent missives today. What do they say?"

"They state that the king grants the Jews in every city permission to gather and defend their lives. If any people or province threatens them, the Jews may destroy, kill, and exterminate its armed force, children, and women, and take their possession for plunder, on a single day, the thirteenth of Addaru," he recites by rote. He must have helped Mordechai oversee the scribes charged with writing the documents.

"Is all that necessary?" I balk.

"It is, for the nations to know what they risk to lose if they insist on attacking the Jews. We shall send unofficial messages to the Jewish communities not to take any spoils; our only objective is to survive, to overcome those who wish our extinction."

"Will the Jews listen?"

"We certainly hope so. Mordechai is confident."

"I see," I murmur, biting my bottom lip. "What reports are you receiving regarding the morale of the Jews throughout the kingdom? Are they despairing?"

"No Jews have come forward to convert. I believe they are invigorated by Mordechai's new position at court... and by Your Highness."

"Good, that's good," I say under my breath. I had wondered why Mordechai flaunted the white and blue royal robes with the purple linen cloak and the large golden crown; I had thought it ostentatious and very unlike Mordechai, but now I see it will certainly lift the spirit of the Jews and encourage them to be proud of their heritage.

So why do I feel so agitated? I am afraid that as long as the threat of destruction looms over my brethren, I will not know peace.

"If there is anything I can do to continue to inspire them to reconnect and strengthen their faith..."

"Forgive me, Your Highness," Shulamit interrupts. "I believe there is something Her Majesty can do that will prove beneficial to both the people and the queen."

"I am listening."

"Go out into the city; let the people pay homage to the queen they love and respect. What's more, Her Highness will be reassured when she will see that the prevailing mood is favorable and very supportive of the Jews."

Shulamit was right. Sitting in the open *harmamaxae*, watching the women and children greeting me so exuberantly, crying, laughing, eagerly offering their hard-earned valuables, moves me in a way I have not felt in a long time.

We inch forward as the throng of people crushes in, in their desire to catch a glimpse of their queen.

Out of the sea of shouting, gesticulating people, one in particular catches my eye. She vigorously elbows her way to us, her ruddy face determined. I smile, a wave of nostalgia washing over me. *Nashiram!* How I've missed her, and the world I used to live in, what now feels like many lifetimes ago.

"My queen!" she pants. "May you be blessed! Her Majesty might recall this lowly servant used to—"

"Impudent woman! How dare you address Her Majesty so!" shouts a guard, about to lunge at her.

"Please," I assert, motioning to the guard to stop. "Allow me."

I reach out and grab her hands. "Nashiram, how could I ever forget you?" I say, holding her hands in a warm grip. "How have you been?"

Nashiram chokes up, and perhaps, for the first time in her life, is at a loss for words.

The years have been kind to her; she is the same Nashiram I have left behind nearly a decade ago. Her face is a bit rounder, and rough as always. Her squinty eyes have not lost their sparkle, and now they stare at me, brimming with tears.

"Ishtar, my beau—my queen!" she bumbles. "Are they not feeding you well at the palace? I must have a talk with my cousins who work in the kitchens, I have to tell them what and how my queen likes her food…" She rambles on. The guards fume, barely restrained, as I hold on to her hands, my heart swelling.

"Don't you, my queen, worry about a thing! No one is going to hurt or lift a finger against your people, if I have a say in it. Your people are my people!" Nashiram forgets herself as she delves into one of her passionate orations. I worry that the guards are not going to be able to contain their indignation any longer, so I pat Nashiram's hands to reel her back into reality, and gently let her go.

I look behind me to find that Nashiram has remained rooted to her spot, her hands in mid-air, as I had left them, staring blankly. I smile to myself, knowing she will recover shortly. I am certain, knowing her, that she will use "the-hands-that-were-held-warmly-by-Her-Majesty-the-queen" as a prerogative to spike up the price of her goods, or at least to impress upon her customers what a bargain they are receiving.

I am heartened to see the positive attitude the people of Shushan have towards the Jews, and pleased the Jews seem revitalized, unapologetically displaying their prayer shawls and *Teffilin* in the streets, proud of their heritage.

HaShem will certainly help.

*   *   *

A scorching summer sun, a pale winter moon, and before I know it, Addaru is upon us. Green and white drapes sway in the breeze, the orchard spreading endlessly across from us. Achashverosh sits warily on the couch, swirling the wine in his golden rhyton, the food before us untouched. I sit composed, watching the horizon blush with its setting sun, with a calm demeanor that belies the turmoil that rages inside.

"You have not touched the food," Achashverosh notes, perhaps for the first time since I've become queen.

"Yes, Your Majesty, I am fasting today."

"Why?"

"My people are in danger, fighting for their lives. I pray for mercy. May the Creator of the world bring this conflict to a peaceful, successful end."

"I have ordered reports to be brought immediately," he tells me. "We shall soon know."

With a click of heavy boots, a scruffy, sweaty guard kneels, waiting to report.

"Tell me what you know," Achashverosh orders, waving his hand.

"Your Majesty, in the capital, the battle still rages. The Jews have killed five hundred men. Ten officers of the court, Haman's sons, have also been executed."

"Five hundred!" he blurts, letting loose a litany of imprecations. "In Shushan alone?"

"Yes, Your Majesty."

I had hoped that the positive mood I had experienced in the city would mirrors today's' numbers. I am grieved it is not so.

"What are the Jews' casualties?"

"None, Your Highness."

Praised be HaShem.

"Five hundred…" he rumbles. "Have I been living in a cove of snakes?" he mutters to himself, his anger surging.

"If I may…" I ask Achashverosh. He waves his hand to grant me permission to talk, while grunting and scowling.

"What is the current situation?" I inquire, gesturing the guard to answer.

"Haman's force has been crippled, but it is still fighting."

"My king," I venture. "Will you allow the Jews to continue defending themselves?"

"If in the capital alone they have slain five hundred men, what have they done throughout the rest of my kingdom?" he rants, a fire burning in his eyes, the eyes of a madman. "What will they want next? Their Temple? My Throne?"

His accusations slap me across the face with resounding force. I fall on my knees, trembling. He may as well have a rock instead of a heart. *Has he learnt nothing?*

"My king," I implore, losing any pretense at decorum. "Have I not been a good queen to you? Have I ever given you reason to doubt my loyalty? Have I ever given you reason to believe me cruel and not compassionate?" I cry shamelessly. "The rules that make Jews different are what made me. Surely you must appreciate that I am a product of that."

Achashverosh softens his stance. "Whatever you ask for, Queen Esther, will be given to you," he concedes. "What is your request?"

"If it pleases the king, let tomorrow, too, be granted to the Jews of Shushan to do the same as today's decree, and let Haman's ten sons hang on the gallows."

Another day for the Jews to kill their enemy, so that a day like this may never happen in the future. Snakes will not be grateful to have been spared, they will bite the moment they have the chance. If I am to be merciful now towards the cruel ones, I shall end up being cruel to the ones in need of compassion. I shan't repeat my great grandfather's mistake. I will not have compassion for the likes of Haman, whose hate is without reason, without cause. The Amalekite hatred.

When the Jews came out of Egypt, they were attacked, unprovoked, by the nation of Amalek, even though no other nation dared to at that time. Mighty Egypt had just been defeated, and all the nations had heard of the incredible miracles that had occurred at the hand of the G-d of Israel. Yet Amalek, knowing that failure was almost certain, still attacked Israel.

It is a frightening concept, to hate with such fervor. That even when there is nothing to be gained, one would insist on harming the object of his hate. Nothing one can do will ease this sort of hate, it will only foster it, for there is no basis for it. It simply is. And it is evil. Perhaps it is for this reason that HaShem declared His throne could not be complete until Amalek, and what it represents, would be utterly eradicated.

"Let a law be passed in Shushan for tomorrow, as the queen wishes," Achashverosh proclaims. "Mordechai, I trust you will see to it."

"It shall be done, Your Majesty."

"And those traitors' bodies, Parshandatha, Dalphon, Aspatha, Poratha, Adalia, Aridatha, Parmashta, Arisai, Aridai and Vaizatha, should be hung on the same gallows as their father Haman," he orders. "Conveniently, Haman made it tall enough to hold all of them at the same time," he grumbles. The thought that Haman may have made that same gallows so prominent to hang the king himself on it, makes Achashverosh boil over with rage. "Let everyone see the fate of who betrays the king."

"It shall be done, Your Majesty."

CHAPTER TWELVE

Kitvuni ledorot, record me for all generations

(Megilla 7a)

*H*aShem is near to all who call Him with sincerity.

I bring the rhyton to my lips and sip on the thick, sweet wine, savoring the warm sensation as it spreads down my throat to my chest.

Generation to generation will praise Your works, and recite Your mighty deeds.

It is too soon to find out what happened in the more distant satrapies. It will take a few months at least, even with the fastest dromedaries, but I believe it will mirror the miraculous victory we witnessed here in Shushan. Not one Jewish casualty, not one thread taken as spoils. I am overwhelmed with gratitude.

Your greatness I shall sing, and bless Your holy name forever and ever.

This should become a day to remember and celebrate for all posterity.

The chamberlain interrupts my musing with his soft, raspy basso. "Your Highness, the *ganzabara* has been summoned, as per your request." He bows his smooth shaven head, revealing behind him the thin, hunched treasury-keeper.

"Raibaya," I acknowledge him with a nod. "As I am celebrating the averting of a massacre, and the people are resting from battle, I want you to draw from my estate and bestow gifts of prepared food to the populace in Shushan."

"As you wish, Your Highness," he says with his usual impenetrable tone. Throughout the years that I have dealt with Raibaya, not once have I gleaned as much as a hint as to what his thoughts may have been on the dispensing of the royal treasures. People say that wealth doesn't affect me, but they are wrong. It may not tempt me, but it pains me to see the outrageous, wanton waste that occurs every day at the expense of the suffering masses. Raibaya, on the other hand, seem apathetic to it all, at least, outwardly. I suppose that is precisely what makes him the man for the job.

"Everyone is to benefit. However, I want you to make a point to distribute as much as possible among the poor, without them knowing you are targeting them specifically. I don't want them to feel like they are being given charity. This is a gift rich and poor alike are receiving. Do you understand what I mean?"

"Quite clearly, Your Highness," he answers in the same detached voice.

"Thank you. You may go then."

The reports brought from the most distant provinces in the Persian Empire confirmed what I already knew in my heart. Though thousands of the enemy fell, not one Jew was harmed, and the spoils were left untouched.

Mordechai and I both strongly feel this event should be celebrated for all generations, for it was more than our lives being spared. It brought to the fore and renewed our commitment to HaShem, though we still live in exile, and though our Temple Mount still lies in ruin.

I lean on the column of the Apadna, the smooth marble cold under my hand. Wet wind howls through the vast hall, as rain pours furiously outside.

I much prefer my spot under the cedar trees as my meeting place with Mordechai and Nechemia, but when the weather imposes itself so fiercely, I am left with indoor public spaces, like the Apadna. No matter how vast and impressive, it still suffocates me. The Bisan at least affords me an impression of liberty.

The rhythmic clicking of purposeful steps reverberates in the Apadna, and I turn to see Mordechai, white and blue robes flowing, and Nechemia, closing upon me.

They nod. "Your Highness."

Mordechai hands me a rolled parchment, a smile dancing in his eyes. "I wrote down the story of our trials and redemption. I would like Her Highness to tell me what she thinks."

I can only peruse it briefly, but even without more analytical attention, it is obviously a work divinely inspired.

"May I hold it for a day or more?"

"Most certainly."

"I only skimmed it, but is there no mention of HaShem's Holy Name?"

"Your Highness is as sharp as ever," Mordechai exclaims, beaming. Then he remembers himself. "Indeed," he says, clearing his throat. "I have purposely left it out, as Achashverosh will most likely adopt it for his own Chronicles, and switch the Holy Name for his own god."

"I imagine you left out some other details of the story, details that would make the king uncomfortable. Is the story not compromised then?"

"Let's just say that a discerning eye will be able to read between the lines."

I nod, eager at the prospect of uncovering the secret hints and codes. "Have you shown it to the Sanhedrin?"

"Yes, as part of my appeal to have Purim established as a Holiday for the all the Jewish people, not just the ones living in the Persian Empire, and for all eternity."

"Purim?"

"Yes, I find it a most suitable name. Haman believed that casting a puru would direct the Jews to an unchangeable destiny, and the Jews proved that as long as we cling to our One and Only, we'll always succeed."

"There is no mention of Darius. I am curious as to why?"

"This is the story of our salvation. Haman threatened us, and HaShem saved us. The Almighty, Blessed-Be-He, brought the cure before the malady, by removing the wicked Vashti and establishing you as queen. Everything else that happened in our lives is part of another puzzle of His Master Plan."

I nod, my mind swirling in memories past. I have a feeling I will find many hidden treasures, pearls of wisdom, buried beneath the lines of this letter.

"You want people to gather and recount the story by reading this letter?"

"Yes."

"There should be more."

"Of course, feasting and drinking wine, like other holidays."

My heart starts racing as my mind reels. "How about sending gifts of prepared food to the poor, so that they, too, could properly celebrate," I propose. The joy to be felt on this Purim day has to be pure and perfect. I shall not allow any circumstances to mar it at the slightest. Moreover, I wish for the feeling of friendship and unity that prevailed in the aftermath of the war, to be reenacted every year, for eternity. Giving gifts and sharing with friends would probably do.

"Gifts of prepared food should be exchanged among friends," I suggest. "Rich and poor alike, so the charity given won't be felt as charity."

Mordechai's eyes twinkle with pride.

"I want this letter to be part of the Holy Scriptures!" I declare, euphoric.

Mordechai sobers up and looks down, stroking his snowy beard pensively.

"Why?" I ask, sensing his hesitation.

"I will appeal it, but I have a feeling it will be denied."

"Why?"

"I don't enjoy the same popularity with the Jewish Court as I do at the Persian Court."

"How so?"

"Some of the sages feel it is wrong of me to be a statesman. They consider politics a waste of time that should be dedicated to Torah instead."

"Should you resign?"

"No, I understand their opinion, but it doesn't change the fact I believe I ought to be in this position right now. Though Achashverosh favors me right now, he is fickle and unreliable. I can best help my brethren by being Viceroy. It is the right thing to do."

"Then I will make the appeal myself," I assert. "My story has to be told for future generations."

There are times when humility has no place. I have looked the enemy in the eye; I have seen the hatred up close. It pains me to think it, but this is not the end. There will come a time, and time yet again, when a Haman will rise, and perhaps the Jews will forget once more their bond to HaShem. Let them read my story and know that no matter what the circumstances, HaShem is the answer. Returning to commitment to HaShem is the only way to salvation, not putting faith in the presiding authority.

But there is another reason I wish my story to be remembered for posterity. A desire buried deep within, raw, visceral. I dare not utter it, for part of me abhors even entertaining such thoughts. But as I look at Darius, this sentiment painfully resurfaces. This story, and the part I played in it, will be my eternal legacy, my living progeny; not my son, whom I love very much, for he won't carry on my Jewish heritage. Let no Jewish girl ever aspire to a heathen's throne because of me. I was brought here by force, by the Hand of HaShem, for the Jewish people.

*   *   *

Nechemia greets me, his melodious voice doleful. "Blessing unto you, Your Highness."

"What news do you bring me regarding my appeal?"

"The sages still oppose it," he says, stroking his scraggly beard.

"What reasons are they giving?"

"There is concern that rejoicing over our enemies' downfall will elicit resentment and hostility from the nations."

"Is there more?"

"Because we have a tradition from King Solomon not to have in the Scriptures more than three stories concerning the elimination of Amalek, they feel they need a Scriptural basis to incorporate your story, too."

I nod frustrated, drumming my fingers onto my forehead, as I do when the answer I seek eludes me.

"Your Highness," Nechemia ventures apologetically. "Times are changing, prophecy is not what it used to be…Your story will be read far and wide, of that I am certain, but the sages don't deem it *necessary* to be incorporated into Scriptures. It is understandable why the sages hesitate to—"

I swallow an impulsive retort and raise the palm of my hand. "I thank you, Nechemia. I have heard all that I need to hear."

As I have learned from Mordechai, I shall deliberate carefully over the concerns of the sages, and then I shall find the scriptural basis they require, for my story is much more than just a story, and it *must* be preserved for generations to come.

"May I humbly suggest Her Highness refrain from staying up all night, poring over the Scriptures…" Nechemia says quietly, looking away.

"How did you—"

"Your humble servant only guessed," he defends, his lips twitching into a smile. "A restorative sleep brings good counsel."

I nod.

"May HaShem crown you with success."

The morning sun is peeking through distant mountains, glowing orange in the bright blue sky. Nechemia was right. I slept deeply and the morning found me reinvigorated and reborn, like the sun. I pore over the scrolls, looking for inspiration.

"Peace upon Your Highness," Nechemia's greeting tears me away from my contemplations. "Your humble servant awaits your directives."

I carefully roll up the scrolls, bring them to my lips, and then gently wrap them in a green satin.

"I believe that you, as have I, read the letter Mordechai wrote, describing all the events that lead to our salvation. It masterfully conveys what it must without offending the Crown's sensibilities, but without omitting important details either. Truly, it is divinely inspired, prophetic, even."

He nods in agreement.

"There is no cause for concern that rejoicing over Haman's downfall will antagonize the nations, as this event is common knowledge, and it has been recorded in the Royal Chronicles."

I take a deep breath, containing the overwhelming desire to persuade the Sanhedrin.

"As for a scriptural basis for allowing Mordechai's letter to become part of the Holy Writings, I don't know for sure, however... as I was poring over the Book of Moses, I came upon this verse: *Inscribe this as a memorial in the book*. Of course, it is HaShem's command to record in the Torah the infamous incident of Amalek's attack on Israel. But these words tugged at my heart. Indeed, my feelings could not have been expressed more pointedly. This is *my* petition, *my* plea. You know everything I have endured, I have done so only for the sake of our people. HaShem is my witness that I have never enjoyed nor abused my power as queen. This petition, too, is not motivated by selfish desires but for the sake of Israel. That my story may impart them with the wisdom and courage they will need in the future. To grant my story eternity, inscribe it as a memorial in the Book."

Silence follows, one charged with so much energy and feeling that it is deafening.

"Your Highness," Nechemia whispers, bowing his head, his eyes glistening. "I shall report your plea. May HaShem grant the desires of your heart."

He takes his leave, engrossed in thought.

By the Grace of HaShem, the sages accepted my petition.

On the first anniversary of our miraculous salvation, Mordechai and I celebrated, as did all Jews throughout the Empire and beyond. A day of rejoicing, feasting, sharing, and recounting the divine providence that brought about our salvation.

My heart is full.

EPILOGUE

Many daughters have done worthily, but you have surpassed them all.

(Proverbs 31:29)

Another fly falls victim to the arid summer night. The unforgivable heat seems more burdensome tonight, and even Radushnamuya's vigorous fanning is not abating its heavy presence. My senses are dulled, and Maimuna's rhythmic puffs have me vacillate from awake to a dream-like state.

Shifra erupts into my chamber, face ashen, eyes bulging. "Your Highness!"

"What happened?" I inquire, alarmed. But Shifra can only stare at me whimpering. "Shifra, speak up at once!" I order. It is unnerving to see the usually calm Shifra in such a state of disarray and panic.

"The—the king has been assassinated!" she yells, trembling, alternating from whimpering to giggling nervously.

As if I were dipped in a frozen river, I lose my breath. Blood drains from my face, and my feet give way. My maidservants rush to my aid.

"Da—Da—Darius!" I heave, struggling to regain my bearings. "We need to protect Darius," I call out, fear gripping my soul.

I start for the doors, but the chamberlains bar my exit.

"It is not safe for Her Majesty," they say firmly, though they bow their heads humbly. "Please, we cannot allow any harm to befall Her Highness."

"The Crown Prince?"

"We shall safeguard the Crown Prince."

I fall on my bed, my heart in a frenzied gallop. *Please, keep him safe.*

Then I notice Shifra, coiled in a corner, hugging knees to chest, rocking feverishly, making an animal-sounding whimper. My wits restored, I gather my girls on my bed, hold their hands, and together, we recite King David's soothing words of song.

> *HaShem, hear my voice as I call; be gracious to me and answer me. You have been my help; do not abandon me nor forsake me. Hurry to my aid, o, HaShem, my salvation. I place my trust in Your kindness, my heart will rejoice in Your deliverance.*

I am strengthened by them. I place my trust in HaShem.

*   *   *

I shield my eyes from the blazing sun, as I stand, with my retinue, to bid farewell to my son, the soon-to-be-crowned King of Persia. Astride his magnificent gray mare, crimson mantle flowing, he looks much older than his nearly seven years of age.

I shall not join him as he journeys to Pasargadae, where he will have royal initiation by the priests. I cannot pretend it will not pain me when they invoke their pagan gods.

"May the Creator guard your steps and lead you to success," I wish him, looking into his sparkling dark eyes. "When you reach Pasargadae, you will lay aside your purple robes and put on the robes King Cyrus used to wear before he became king—"

"Yes, Duksis Mother," Darius interjects respectfully, but with an edge of impatience in his voice. "I shall then eat cake of figs, chew some terebinth, and drink a cup of sour milk. I have been instructed well on my ceremonial duties, do not worry, Mother."

"I do not worry; you shall perform splendidly, I am sure. I only wish that as King Cyrus did, you, too, shall allow the Jews to return to Jerusalem and build their Holy Temple," I bow with reverence.

He smiles. "I know, I know, it is not the first time I have heard it, Mother," he replies softly. "But, I won't be able to do much for another year at least."

"Do you not officially accept the conferment of privileges and functions, when you stand before your subjects with the upright purple tiara, the scepter in your right hand, and the lotus blossom in your left?"

"Yes I do, officially. In reality, I cannot assume the Crown's duties until a year after Father's passing. That is the law. But I promise I will fulfill your desire." With a quick tug at the mare's rein, he approaches and extends his hand to me. "Your people are my people, too."

I grab his hand and kiss it. "Bless you, my son."

*   *   *

I take in a deep breath of fall-crisp air. The dried leaves float about before carpeting the Bisan with their graceful colors.

"You have called for me, Your Highness?" Mordechai stands by the cedar trees, casting a shadow behind himself. The sun glimmers softly on his face, giving him the aura of an angel.

"Please, have a seat," I say, inviting him to sit on the couch opposite mine.

Mordechai demurs, and remains standing.

I sigh, gathering courage for what I am about to request. "Will you join the Jews journeying to Jerusalem?"

"I fear not, there is still much that I am needed for here in Shushan."

"It has always been your dream to see the Temple standing again in its splendor."

"True."

"I want you to go," I breathe, hiding the tremor in my voice. "I know how much you want to, and I don't want to be what holds you back."

Mordechai lowers his eyes, remains silent, his posture resolute.

"You need not worry about me," I persist. "I shall move to the palace in Hagmatana, one of my estates, far from the political intrigues of Shushan. I shall have more room to do as I please, away from prying eyes. And I trust my son, King Artachshasta, will rule fairly."

Mordechai's eyes are moist and sad, but his voice is steady and strong. "I will stay by your side."

"You must go to our Holy Land," I insist. "Then you will come back and tell me of the heavenly harmonies the Levites sing, and the smells and sights of the Beit Hamikdash."

"You can see and hear them for yourself," he replies, smiling. "It is not uncommon for a queen dowager to travel to pay tributes to her G-d."

"True," I concede. Since Achashverosh's passing, my prison walls have relented somewhat, though I am still not accustomed to it. I know I will never be able to go back to how things were before. I am still queen, and there are rules and expectations to meet. According to Torah law, I can never go back to Mordechai as a wife. Perhaps I am afraid that tasting a little bit of freedom may leave me thirsting for more that's unattainable. But Mordechai is right. If offered a small space to breathe, I should take advantage of it.

"Whatever happens, I could not live with myself, knowing I had prevented you from fulfilling your dream. You must promise me you will go to the Land of Israel."

"Whatever happens," he says, his soft voice unambiguous. "I promise you will be buried next to me. You will have a place next to mine in the World to Come."

I pale, and tears spring out with an involuntary gasp. There is nothing I could have wished for more, but I dared not ask for it, nor did I know if I could.

"You—you promise?" I whisper.

"I promise."

"Amen," I cry. I know they are not empty words or hopeful wishes. A promise from Mordechai is a certainty.

"Rachel, our fore-mother, sacrificed her eternal resting place next to her beloved for the sake of her children, but you, Esther, have already sacrificed your life in this world. That is why you will be next to me in the World to Come."

"You have comforted me, Mordechai," I choke up, tears flowing unabashed. "You have comforted me."

*   *   *

Another letter has arrived from Shushan, detailing my son's rulership and wisdom. Shulamit's voice floats in the chamber, as she reads the updates that Nechemia faithfully writes to me. I am heartened he is still by my son's side, and that my son trusts and confides in him.

A fit of dry coughing rattles my weak, tired body. It is a weariness that is not only physical. My soul is weary. I have lived to see Jeremiah's prophecy fulfilled, the Beit Hamikdash standing in its former glory. I am gratified at the annual celebration of Purim, the commemoration of our salvation. It shall thrive through the ages and never be forgotten.

I lie on my bed, drifting now and again from reality. I stare at the blue curtains hanging elegantly above me, changing shade as they fold about sun-kissed bright spots.

Shulamit kneels at my side, whimpering quietly as she dabs a wet cloth on my forehead.

She has matured into a beautiful woman since that fateful day in the capital's market.

I reach for her hand and pat it reassuringly. "My daughter, do not fret, I feel fine," I lie, smiling feebly.

She nods, sniffling.

Another fit of coughing explodes in my chest, choking me.

Shulamit lets out a cry of consternation. "Mistress," she blubbers, looking at the blood-stained cloth I hold in my hand. "What will I do without you?"

"I am...so grateful...to have had you at my side," I say, panting. "I have...one last request of you..."

"Your wish is my command."

"Promise...promise me...you will do whatever it takes...to bury me next to Mordechai."

"HaShem is my witness, I will carry out your wish, no matter what the cost."

I sink deeper into the bed, releasing her hand; a weight has lifted from my heart. I sigh, grateful.

Suddenly, the chamber brightens with an otherworldly light, and though my vision is blurred, I notice a crowd of people approaching.

They stride, nay, they glide, with a stately bearing, radiating serenity and a love so overpowering, I can hardly contain it. As they draw nearer, I recognize them, though I have never seen them before. My father, my mother, and at their head, tall and handsome, my great-grandfather, King Shaul.

They have come to accompany me to Heaven.

The air has filled with the sweet fragrance of myrtle and citrus. I inhale deeply, filling my lungs with my favorite scent, and it's effortless, painless.

King Shaul is radiant, warmth pouring from his smile. He looks at me, proud eyes shining. "Rabot Banot asu chail veat alit al kulana."

Many daughters have done worthily, but you have surpassed them all.

My heart swells. I stifle a sob, overwhelmed.

I am faintly aware of my girls and their wailing sounds, for I am enraptured by a heavenly melody that is carrying me further away from my surroundings.

King Shaul extends his hand, beckoning me. "It is time, my daughter."

I accept his hand, smiling.

As if gifted with wings, I spring into flight.

At last.

Free.

AUTHOR'S NOTES

I t is my fervent wish that you, dear reader, have been touched by Esther as I have been. As I read Esther's story in my literary group, someone challenged, "Shouldn't she be seduced by the wealth and power? She is human after all." Before I could respond, someone else interjected, "No, she's far too noble for that."

If I am to be faulted for portraying Esther as "too good", I take full responsibility. She was human, but one who transcended our basest instincts. For that, she is lauded as our heroine. I have been lucky in my life to have met such a person, the Lubavicher Rebbe, Menachem Mendel Schneerson. His wife as well, and his mother and great-grandmother (through their writings) were the models by which I was able to give Esther a voice. I thought, in modern terms, how would a woman, married to a holy man like the Rebbe, feel prisoner in an Arafat's "palace". I couldn't bear the thought. How would, then, someone still exude charisma in such a depressing situation? These were the questions I asked myself in attempting to speak for Esther. In doing so, I came to a new appreciation for Esther and how I ought to address traumatic events in my own personal life. I learned from her to let go of what you cannot control, and to allow HaShem to be in control, trusting HaShem only wants what's good for us.

I thank HaShem for the people who diligently gathered together sources of commentaries by renowned G-d-fearing Jewish scholars, the Talmud and Midrash in one book (or two), thereby saving me a lot of time, which, as a home-schooling mother of seven, can be very scarce.

There were times I went to the primary source to check the context, but I will refer to the books I have used in general, and if the reader wishes, he/she can check the original sources quoted in these books.

I have purposefully chosen to omit putting in numbers for the end notes, as I believe it to be distracting.

There is a discrepancy of approximately 150 years between the secular and the Jewish account of the Persian empire.

While I have chosen to use the traditional Jewish dates, as this novel is written from the traditional Jewish perspective and because Jewish chronology makes a stronger case for historical accuracy, I also have "borrowed" some facts from secular accounts.

(To further your knowledge on the different chronologies, look up: *Centuries in Darkness* by Peter James; Rutgers University Press, 1993, p. 318. *History of the Jewish People: The Second Temple Era*, Artscroll Publication, an appendix in the back. www.starways.net/lisa/essays/heifetzfix.html)

There are two opinions in the Jewish tradition as to who Achashverosh was. One holds that he was a son of Cyrus, and grandson to Darius the Mede, the other that he was a wealthy opportunist, not of royal blood, who bought his way to the throne.

I chose to identify Achashverosh as Xerxes I (which is the Greek equivalent of the Persian Khshayarsha), as in my opinion he resembles most the Biblical Ahasuerus, changing some details from the secular accounts. For example, I have Xerxes be son of royalty but not legitimate to the line of succession to "satisfy" both opinions stated above. (Son of Darius and a concubine and not firstborn.)

The historical backround is adapted from Meam Loez, pages xii,xiii,xiv.

Mordechai was quite old when he married Esther (possibly in his sixties) and there is a Midrash that says Esther was adopted as a baby by a single Mordechai (Genesis Raba 30:8). Because Mordechai was a respected member of the Great Sanhedrin, and was known with the appellative of Hayehudi, the Jew, implying that he was Torah-abiding, there arise the problem of yichud (being alone in the same house with a member of the opposite gender not being closely related). Given that the laws of yichud were instituted by King David, we must assume Mordechai abided by them. The easiest solution was for Mordechai to have married, the wife providing the solution to the yichud problem, and it isn't a contradiction that we don't know of such a wife because she was inconsequential and Scripture only gives us those details of their lives that pertain to teachings for us.

Mordechai's name being Pethachia (Menachot 65a)

Vashti's cruelty and punishment (Megilla 12)

Haman's hand in rescinding the decree of Cyrus to allow the Temple to be built (Aggadas Esther 5:9)

Mordechai meeting the children from school. (Esther Rabba 7:13)

Whenever possible, the words I put in Esther's mouth are extracted from Psalms or Scriptures or maxims from later sages. The assertion of Esther that a bad prophecy can be averted by repenting, but a good one will always come true is from the 13 Principles of Faith expounded by Maimonides. Likewise, "Why-is-the-path-of-the-wicked-peaceful" is a sentiment found in Jeremiah 12:1 and Job 21:7.

Woe to us, for we have sinned. Restore us to You, oh, HaShem, that we may be restored. Renew our days as of old. (Lamentation 5:16, 21)

Why have You done bad to this people? (Exodus 5:22)

You shall not make for yourself a sculptured image or any picture of that which is in the heavens above, or the earth below. (Exodus 20:4)

*"Just as I leap toward you but cannot touch you, so may all my enemies be unable to touch me (*Talmud, Tractate Soferim 20:2; Shulchan Aruch, Orach Chaim 426:2*)*

The righteous will grow tall like a cedar, planted in the House of HaShem, they shall blossom and be fruitful even in old age; they shall be full of sap and freshness—to declare HaShem is just. (Psalms 92:12)

Tzadka mimeni.(Genesis 38:26. Judah recognizing Tamar was right)

Out of the depths I call to You, HaShem, hearken to my pleas. If You were to preserve iniquities, My God, who could survive? But forgiveness is with You, that You may be held in awe. (Psalm130:1,3,4)

God of Israel, Creator of the world, Who has dominion for eternity! Help your lowly maidservant, for I am an orphan, without father and mother. Save Your flock from these enemies who have risen up against us. Father of orphans! I beseech You to stand by the right hand of this orphan, who has placed her trust in Your Loving kindness. Grant me mercy before this man, for I fear him. Cast him down before me, for You cast down the haughty. (Esther Rabba 8:7)

Israel, put your hope in HaShem, for with Him there is kindness; with Him there is abounding deliverance. And He will redeem Israel from all its iniquities. (Psalm 130:7,8)

Though I walk in the valley of the shadow of death, I will fear no evil, for You are with me. (Psalm 23:4)

My help comes from HaShem, Maker of heaven and earth. (Psalm 121:2)

Blessed is my Rock Who delivered me from the man of violence. I will sing to HaShem for he has dealt kindly with me. (Psalms 144:1; 18:49; 13:6)

HaShem is near to all who call Him with sincerity. Generation to generation will praise Your works, and recite Your mighty deeds. Your greatness I shall sing, and bless Your holy name forever and ever. (Psalm 145:18, 4, 21)

HaShem, hear my voice as I call; be gracious to me and answer me. You have been my help; do not abandon me nor forsake me. Hurry to my aid, o HaShem, my salvation. I place my trust in Your kindness, my heart will rejoice in Your deliverance. (Psalms 27:7, 9; 38:23; 13:6)

My G-d, why Have You forsaken me and Esther's thoughts as she approaches Achashverosh are from Psalms 22, which is said to have been a tribute to Esther. (see Rashi)

*For He desires His way…*is from Psalms 37:23 and its interpretation is from Branches of the Chassidic Menorah II, page 25.

Darius ripping the flower and being reprimanded by his mother is an adaption from the writings and talks of Rabbi Yosef Yitzchak of Lubavich. (Likkutei Dibburim; vol 1, pg 168-170)

The dream Esther had is my own creation I used as a plot device to foreshadow the coming events, though the concept of rectifying Shaul's mistake is found in Midrash.

Though prayers and blessing were formalized later on by the Sanhedrin, because Mordechai was part of the original Sanhedrin, it is safe to assume some of the liturgy was already in use. The Midrash tells us that our Matriarch Sara used to light Shabbat candles (Genesis Rabba 24:67) and it praises Esther for wanting to emulate her Matriarch (therefore, she is rewarded with ruling over 127 regions, as many as Sara's years).(Esther Rabba 58:3)

Haman's letter (in the name of King Achashverosh) is from The Book of Our Heritage, pgs 69-72.

Esther's reasoning for inviting Haman at the banquet: The Book of Our Heritage, pgs 67,68.

Esther's plea to be inscribed in the Torah and the initial sages' opposition is found in Megilla 7a. The Scriptural allowance for the canonization of the Book of Esther is the verse found in Exodus 17:14.

Esther's claim of the prophetic nature of the Book of Esther has resonated throughout the difficult Jewish history of persecution, sometimes with uncanny accuracy.

The Book of Esther lists the ten sons of Haman who were hanged in one day. Three letters in three different sons are written small. They spell out the Hebrew year date (taf-shin-zayin) in which ten Nazi criminals were hanged on October 16th, in 1946, in Nuremberg. Julius Streicher, may his name be blotted out, cried out before his sentence was carried out, "Purim fest 1946."

Because Nechemia seemed to have had a close and warm relationship with Archtashashta (successor to Achashverosh), who sought Nechemia's counsel, asking him to return from Jerusalem (See Nechemia), I thought it natural and likely that the orchestrator of that relationship was Esther.

There was no source I could find that addresses Esther's life after the story of Purim and her passing. However, considering there is a tradition passed down that Esther and Mordechai are both buried in

Hamadan, what used to be Hagmatana or Ecbatana (the "old capital city" where Cyrus presided), I have Esther move to that palace in her later years. I left her burial location open-ended because of an alternate tradition indicating that Esther and Mordechai were brought to Israel for burial, in the Galilean village of Bar'am. What is interesting is that both traditions (whether they are buried in Iran or Israel) hold that Esther and Mordechai are buried together. It is on this basis that I have Mordechai promise Esther a place next to him in the Eternal life.

One late night, in 1942, in Hamadan, the local rabbi was approached by a Muslim who owned a coffe-shop next to Esther's Tomb. "There is a lady trapped in your building, I can hear her cry, why don't you take care of her?" he complained. The rabbi was confused. Usually, Esther's Tomb was kept locked before nightfall, after ensuring everyone had left. He went to investigate, but there was no one to be found. Shaken, the rabbi called the community together. He called for a day of fast and prayer, Queen Esther must be crying for her children, he felt, "let us pray to HaShem for the safety of the Jews." Monavar

Alaghband-Darshi, then a twenty-year-old woman, remembers coming home after the long night and day spent in the synagogue, turning on the short wave radio to find out that Germany had suffered their first defeat at Stalingrad and were beginning their retreat.

I heard this story from Monavar's grandson, Farhad Daghighian, who corroborated it with Rabbi Ovadia Nataneli, who was present as a teenager at the time of the event.

The Talmud praises Esther for striving to be like the Matriarchs. Considering Esther was a descendent of Rachel (from the tribe of Benjamin), I found this story movingly echoed Rachel's crying for her children (Jeremiah 31:14. see Rashi)

BIBLIOGRAPHY

Kaplan, Aryeh, trans. *The Book of Esther: MeAm Lo'ez* (New York/Jerusalem: Maznaim Publishing Corporation, 1978).

Kantor, Mattis, *The Jewish Time Line Encyclopedia* (Northvale: Jason Aronson Inc., 1992).

Landy, Yehuda, *Purim and The Persian Empire: A Historical, Archeological, and Geographical Perspective* (Jerusalem/New York: Feldheim Publishers, 2010).

Kitov, Eliyahu, *The Book of Our Heritage: The Jewish Year and Its Days of Significance, vol 2, Adar-Nissan* (Feldheim, 1978).

Rebbetzin Heller, *A Teacher's Treasure, Megillas Esther* (Bais Rivkah Seminary, 1998).

Bogomilsky, Moshe, *Vedibarta Bam: And you shall speak of them, Megillat Esther* (2002)

Kol Menachem Megillah: Commentary and Insights Anthologized from Classic Texts and the Works of the

Lubavitcher Rebbe. Compiled and Adapted by Rabbi Chaim Miller (Kol Menachem, 2010).

Steinsaltz, Adin, *The Essential Talmud* (BasicBooks, 1976).

Winter, Naphtali, *Purim revealed* (Israel Book Shop, 2007).

Wiesehöfer, Josef, *Ancient Persia* (I. B. Tauris, 2001).

Weisberg, Chana, "Esther: Paradigm of Self-Sacrifice" (http://www.chabad.org/2485034 (accessed on February 8, 2015)).